An important message

To the girl with the baby animal eyes:

Try to look out the window of the van as much as you can, and when you have to go to the bathroom, make sure lots of people see you.

If you get a chance to run away, do it.

You're not invisible anymore, at least part of you isn't.

The police are looking for you, and I'm hoping to remember more so I can help.

I won't forget, I promise.

I won't let it go.

Your friend forever,

Anna McConnell

ALSO BY

JOAN BAUER

❀

Tell Me

JOAN BAUER

PUFFIN BOOKS

PUFFIN BOOKS
An Imprint of Penguin Random House LLC
375 Hudson Street
New York, New York 10014

First published in the United States of America by Viking Children's Books,
an imprint of Penguin Young Readers Group, 2014
Published by Puffin Books, an imprint of Penguin Random House LLC, 2015

THE LIBRARY OF CONGRESS HAS CATALOGED THE VIKING CHILDREN'S BOOKS EDITION AS FOLLOWS:
Bauer, Joan, date.
Tell Me / Joan Bauer
pages cm
Summary: Feeling scared and powerless when her father's anger escalates and her parents separate,
twelve-year-old Anna spends the summer with her grandmother and decides to make a difference
when she sees what seems to be a girl held against her will.
ISBN 978-0-451-47033-1 (hardcover)
[1. Fathers and daughters—Fiction. 2. Parents—Fiction. 3. Fear—Fiction.
4. Rescues—Fiction.] I. Title.
PZ7.B32615Te 2014
[Fic]—dc23
2014003708

Puffin Books ISBN 978-0-14-751314-4

Printed in the United States of America

1 3 5 7 9 10 8 6 4 2

Book design by Nancy Brennan

For Evan, who listens

Tell Me

Prologue

This isn't just a story about a girl (me) and my intense training in drama.

It's not just about Things Happening in a Family, either.

You've got to trust me when I tell you, that's just part of it.

Mostly it's about seeing, really seeing, and not telling yourself you didn't see it.

It's about telling what you saw.

And then deciding you've got a bigger role to play.

I'll remember her eyes forever.

Big, scared, baby animal eyes.

And the questions that wouldn't let me go.

Did I see something?

Is a girl in trouble?

What can I do?

What should I do?

I mean . . .

What should anybody do?

This is the story of what I did, along with the amazing people who put themselves out there to help.

—Anna M. McConnell, age 12, Philadelphia

One

I am in the mall dressed like a cranberry, feeling the emotion of the moment.

What do I want to leave them with?

I've been seriously trained to ask this question.

I sit here thinking, and sitting isn't easy because of the outfit I'm wearing. Every time I move, it puffs up.

"We're ready, Anna." That's Lorenzo Lu, my best friend and acting partner.

"I'll be right there. . . ."

What do I want to leave them with?

Sometimes I think in big, fat letters.

I study myself in the scratched mirror. My face is

covered with red makeup, and my lips shine with ruby lipstick. I smooth out my round, red costume, adjust my red gloves, scratch my red tights. I think I'm allergic to these tights. I look at the pile of 20 percent off coupons from the Wide World of Cranberries store and feel a major surge of energy.

I want them to be happy they came.
I want them to know that this cranberry cares.

Lorenzo is wearing jeans, a red and white striped shirt, red socks, white shoes, and a big button that reads, I'M WITH THE CRANBERRY.

I wiggle my hips, aim my voice to the corner of the room. "Do I look fat in this?" My voice echoes back. Very few kids can do this trick.

Lorenzo laughs. "You look fat, Anna, because you are packed with antioxidants."

Antioxidants are major players in the cranberry world.

Lorenzo sighs. His dad is Chinese and his mother is Italian; he's got the best blend in his face. "I wish you didn't have to go."

I know.

Out in the mall, the music starts playing.

I can hear Mr. Dimsdale shout into his microphone, "And now, are you ready for the big fun?"

"Of course they are." I scratch my tights again.

"I might have to go to the bathroom," Lorenzo mentions.

I shake my head at him. The rule of performers everywhere in the galaxy is, *The Show Must Go On.*

"Heeeere she is!"

Lorenzo and I run out into the mall to wild applause.

A little girl shrieks, "Hi, Miss Berry!"

Lorenzo and I move to the beat.

The music makes you want to dance.

One . . .

Two . . .

Three . . .

Four . . .

I raise my hand and do a twirl; Lorenzo gets down and does a break-dance move.

The crowd loves this.

I do a shimmy as Lorenzo takes the mic from Mr. Dimsdale and declares, "For years, the cranberry was taken for granted. . . ."

I slump and look sad.

"For years the cranberry's nutritional contents were known to only a few. . . ."

I look pathetically unappreciated. People laugh.

"But, the truth is now known. . . ."

I jump up and make a noise.

"Cranberries are among the world's healthiest foods!"

I spin around at this news.

"So healthy that an entire store has been dedicated to cranberries in every form."

Ta da!!

I point to the Wide World of Cranberries store and clap my hands.

Then Lorenzo goes off script. "Cranberries," he shouts. "They're not just for UTIs anymore."

Women laugh hard. Fred Dimsdale looks nervous.

"What's a UTI?" a little boy asks his mother.

"Urinary tract infection," the mother says quietly.

Lorenzo has three older sisters and knows about these things. "This," he declares, "is the sale of the century!"

Actually, the store has only been open since April, but you get the idea. I run into the shop and people follow me.

I look at the anti-aging supplement display, bounce my voice there.

"Let's hit it!" I say, and my voice echoes back.

A little boy yells, "How did you do that?"

Years of practice, child. That's the short answer.

I dance with kids. I do the slide. I say, "We're so glad you're shopping with us today!"

When someone buys something, I have to shout, "Antioxidants rule!" It's not an easy line.

But I know how to deliver.

Fred Dimsdale, the owner of the cranberry store, saw me perform one of my most heartbreaking roles as a radish at the Children's Drama Workshop—a lonely, rejected radish singing my heart out—and he was deeply moved.

"Can you play other produce, kid? Something cheerier? I felt your pain with the radish, but . . ."

The song I sang as a radish was written by Charlie Chaplin, a famous mime who made a fortune by saying absolutely nothing, but he wrote a song about how you've got to smile no matter what.

"I can play other produce," I assured him.

The cranberry is a non-singing part, which is fine by

me. I've had some issues singing—my mouth gets dry. I get hoarse and nervous.

But that moment as a singing radish—I sang like I always hoped I could.

Lorenzo and I have been doing four shows a day every weekend since the store opened. Fred Dimsdale offered to extend us through the summer, but I'm not going to be in town.

I've got to go stay with my grandmother in Virginia because of all the things happening in my family.

My mom and dad's marriage isn't doing so well.

"Puffy hug!" I shout, and little kids run up and hug my padding.

I added the hug move last week. Mr. Dez, my drama coach, always says, "Use a part of what you need in the role you're playing."

More and more these days, I really need a good hug.

Fred Dimsdale hands me my check. "You brought the heart of a cranberry to every performance, kid. I'm going to miss you. It won't be the same." He looks over at Jeremy Pearlmutter, who is going to play the cranberry after me. Jeremy is here to observe me doing the act, but so far all he's done is yawn and scratch his neck. He hasn't asked me one question about the experience.

I don't think Jeremy will lose himself in the role.

"Thanks for giving me a job, Mr. Dimsdale."

"Call me when you get back, kid. First thing." He sounds desperate.

"I will." I shake his hand.

I walk to the back of the store, into the little office, and change out of the costume. Usually I wear it home—when a cranberry is walking down the street, people want to know more.

I put the costume on a hanger, use makeup remover to get the red off my face.

In real life, I look nothing like a cranberry.

I'm medium height. I have curly auburn hair that falls in my face. People say I'm pretty. I've got dark brown eyes like my dad.

I used to be closer to my dad than I am now.

Lorenzo and I walk to the escalator.

"Tell me again why you're leaving," he says.

I sigh. "I know it's a bad time for me to go."

Lorenzo throws back his head. "There would never be a good time for you to go. I'm going to have to work in my uncle's drug store this summer, Anna—three days a week—totally exposed to sick people. I mean, if some major viral strain breaks out . . ." Lorenzo squirts antiseptic cleaner on his hands. "And we're going to have to talk about our future! Eighth grade isn't looking good!"

I know that, too. The high school has an after-school drama program, but we're not in high school yet. The middle school has nothing. We're too old for the Children's Drama Workshop. They kick you out on your twelfth birthday into the big, cold world.

We head down the escalator.

I wonder what's going to happen with my parents while I'm away.

I wonder if staying with Mim, my grandmother, is the right thing—maybe my parents need me around and they just don't know it.

Lorenzo puts his hand on my shoulder. "Just remember, Anna, cranberries are the bravest fruit."

I square my shoulders to prove he's right.

We walk to the entrance of the mall. I feel all the mess twisting me up inside. It's easy to pretend everything is fine when you're in a cranberry suit—you can hide from the world because no one can see the real you.

When it's just you and your face and heart out there, it's so much harder.

Two

I walk into my house and try not to look at the table. I told Mom we should have a sheet over it or something.

I do look at it though—our dining room table, on its side, broken.

Everything else in our dining room has been picked up. Everything but the memories.

I try to remember the good times we had in this room—the holidays, my birthday parties, the time Dad and I decorated the dining room like Hawaii for Mom's birthday, with paper palm trees and huge flowers.

One stupid moment can change everything.

It happened eight days ago when Dad picked me up at the mall after my cranberry gig. Driving with Dad isn't easy.

He was driving too fast, like he always does, when a man in a black sports car cut him off. Dad takes these things personally.

"Dad, remember you're not supposed to—"

He sped after the guy, shouting out the window.

"Dad! It was, tops, an SDM." That stands for Small Dumb Move. Lorenzo and I created anger management phrases to help my father get a grip. They don't always work.

The guy in the black car made The Ultimate Bad Gesture. My father went radioactive.

"JDT!" I hollered (Jerks Do This).

But the anger was driving Dad and wouldn't let go. He got too close to the guy's car.

"Dad, pull over!"

The guy in the black car almost hit us. Dad leaned on the horn. The guy pulled over; Dad did, too. The man in the black car got out, screaming. He stormed over to us, glared at me, and hollered, "What are you?"

I was still in the fruit suit.

"Don't yell at my daughter!"

"I'm a cranberry!" I screamed. "A helpless cranberry. I'm just trying to get home."

The guy stared at me. At the Children's Drama Workshop, one of the things we learned was, *Use the pain.*

I shrieked, "And I have to go to the bathroom!"

A police car drove up. "What's going on?" the cop demanded.

I raised my hand. "Permission to get out of the car, officer."

The cop nodded. I got out, waddled over, and gave the man and the policeman a 20 percent off coupon.

I mentioned the bathroom again, told them to stop by the store, waddled back to the car.

The angry man snarled, "Where do you think you're going, ace?"

The cop pocketed his coupon. "The cranberry has to go to the bathroom."

I'm still trying to decide if I bribed a policeman.

Dad pulled out; his eyes were fierce. "Nobody does that to me, Anna. Nobody!"

It was like opening a dam. All the water came rushing out.

Back home, Mom didn't let Dad cool down. She got right in his face. "What happened?"

Big mistake. That made him madder.

So mad, he turned over the dining room table. Dishes broke. The vase of flowers crashed to the floor.

Mom screamed, "Brian, what is the matter with you?"

That was the Big Question we'd been asking all year.

Dad left.

Left Mom standing there.

Left me trying to get out of my cranberry suit.

Left Peanut, my dog, shaking in the corner.

Mom started crying. "Enough. It's enough."

The next day Mom and I went to see Jen, our family therapist. Mom announced, "Your dad and I . . . well, we're going to be separated for awhile."

I'd been expecting this, but the news still hit like a baseball smashing a window.

"And, Anna, I'm thinking about . . . well, not just thinking, I've made the decision to stay with Uncle Barry for a while." Barry is her brother. He lives in New Jersey. His wife collects miniature eggs with little forest animals peeking out of them. They're all over the house. Mom hates it there.

I looked at my hands. "Where am I going to be?"

I felt this rumble in my chest like a monster was in there. I had to bend over, even though I was sitting. I put my head between my legs.

Mom said, "Breathe, honey," like I was sitting there

with my head between my legs holding my breath.

"Slow in, slow out," Jen added.

I got the rhythm of that. I sat up.

Then we talked about me staying with my grand-mother for "awhile."

Nobody defined "awhile."

"Anna, the flower festival is in a few weeks," Mom mentioned.

Mim lives in Rosemont, this tiny town in Virginia that lives and breathes flowers. The whole town turns out for the flower festival. Tourists come from all over.

I said nothing.

"Honey, your dad needs to get hold of his anger, and while he does that I think he needs for us not to be around. Okay?"

Mim is Dad's mother, but she and Mom are amazingly close. And it's not that I didn't love my grand-mother, but why did my parents want to live someplace without me?

Mom leaned forward. She looked so pale. "This is colossally hard on everybody. I want you to be in a place that's peaceful. I need, honestly, some space to work this through. Okay?"

I shook my head. None of this was okay.

"Certainly, Anna, if you don't want to do this—"

"I don't know what I want! I just heard that my parents are splitting up."

"Separating, Anna. . . ."

I pulled out my phone, went to the dictionary. "Separate," I announced. "To divide, to disunite, to become disconnected or severed."

Jen stepped in. "It's good to define a word, Anna, but sometimes that can label a thing too harshly. Separation can be a step toward divorce, but not always."

Mom leaned forward. "Anna, do you want to stay with me at Barry's?"

I shook my head no, but at least she offered.

We sat there not talking.

Then I asked. I had to.

"Do you love him, Mom?"

She shifted in her chair. "Your dad and I have been married for nineteen years."

"Do you love him?"

Her shoulders sagged. "Honestly, I don't know."

That was my week.

❀   ❀   ❀

I stand in the dining room. My suitcase is packed and by the door. Peanut, my dachshund, isn't sure about anything.

"It's okay, girl."

Peanut knows this is a deep lie.

"All right, it's not exactly okay, but we're going to handle this."

Peanut looks at my suitcase.

"I don't think I'll be gone too long."

She looks at me. Peanut has been my dog for eight years—it's hard to put anything over on her.

"I hope I won't be gone too long."

I see a piece of broken glass on the floor. I pick it up.

Brian, what is the matter with you?

I wonder how anger got so popular—people screaming on TV, ranting on the news, politicians yelling at each other. None of it seems to do much good.

I throw the broken glass into the trash, sit on the floor, and let Peanut crawl in my lap. "I got a card," I tell her.

She sniffs the envelope.

"Does it smell like Lorenzo?" I open the envelope Lorenzo gave me, take out the yellow card. "Yellow is our favorite color, right?"

HAVE AN AMAZING ADVENTURE, ANNA!
COME BACK SOON
OR I'M GOING TO BE IRRITATED!

I smile. Lorenzo is the best friend ever. Inside he wrote:

* pea in a pod
* irritated gerbil
* top of totem pole
* Health Week monkey
* beloved oak tree

These are some of the roles I've played over the years. Lorenzo says every role an actor plays stays with them and makes them stronger.

* comic cupcake
* angry worm

* amazing dancing cranberry
* the lead in Cinderella, the Early Years
* lonely radish

Right now I'm feeling mostly like a lonely radish.

I could sing the "Smile" song, but I don't want to.

Mom comes down the stairs stiffly. "Well, honey, are you ready?"

It won't do any good to mention that I'm not.

We lug my stuff out to the car.

We drop Peanut next door with Mr. Vincenzo, who balances a dog biscuit on his nose, and Peanut hops up to get it. This is their big trick.

I give her a hug. "You be a good dog."

That gets a tail wag.

Mom and I fold our arms across our chests exactly the same way, then we thank Mr. Vincenzo and head out the door.

"'Bye, Peanut."

"Well . . ." Mom doesn't finish the thought. We walk to our car, get in.

Mom sighs, starts the Malibu, and drives down Pine Street toward the Schuylkill Expressway.

HAVE AN AMAZING ADVENTURE, ANNA!
COME BACK SOON
OR I'M GOING TO BE IRRITATED!

I'm not sure about this being an amazing adventure.

I am sure that I need a vacation from my life.

Not a forever vacation, though. A couple of weeks should give my parents enough time to fix things.

I watch the road signs leading us out of Philadelphia to I-76.

I slump in my seat. It's official—the cranberry has left the city.

Three

We've been driving for two hours. Mom is getting emotional.

"I need to say this, Anna. I'm just so sad about all
that's happened, and you know that your dad and I are
going to be seeing Jen regularly while you're gone."

I know that. Uncle Barry's house is an hour from
Philadelphia.

"And I'm hoping you won't worry, honey, because I
know how worry can wear you down."

I bite my thumbnail, not that there's much nail left.

Mom says if I stop biting my nails, she and I can go
get a manicure.

Me, I'm not the manicure type.

"And I've been thinking," Mom adds. "If you feel
dizzy . . ."

"I'll sit down, Mom. Unless, I'm walking across a
busy street, or I'm running away from evil."

"Tell you what. Avoid evil, honey. Got it?"

Got it.

No worry allowed.
No evil allowed.
If I feel dizzy, sit down,
but not in the street.

"Anna, are you listening to me?"

"Yes."

"I just want to make sure—"

"Mom, I want to talk, but could we do it a little later?"

She takes a big breath and nods. "We're making good time."

We're in Baltimore; an hour later, D.C.

Already I miss my life.

I can hear Mr. Dez at the Children's Drama Workshop asking, "So, what are you about?"

You have to know this when you're an actor, because if you don't know that, you can't pull from who you are. You won't make your mark.

No matter what size role you get—and I've had some dinky parts, believe me—you've got to hang onto this:

*There's something that only I can bring to this part,
and I'm going for it.*

Lorenzo and I were the only four-year-olds enrolled
in the Children's Drama Workshop, but we didn't coast
through on adorableness alone. We practiced hard, we
learned our lines, and we worked our way up from playing two peas in a pod (in the world premier of *Jonathan,
Eat Your Vegetables*), to almost starring roles.

My mom and dad came to every performance. Dad
always laughed in the perfect places. He has the best
laugh of any father.

Except for this past year. He's not been laughing much.

I feel a rumble in my chest. I roll down the window
and suck in as much fresh air as I can. I didn't used to
have trouble breathing. I got checked for asthma, but I
don't have that.

When Dad started changing, it got to me—I was
closer to him than to my mom, but anger separates
people. It's a wall that goes up. I kept trying to do
things that would make him feel better, like making
cookies and asking him if he wanted to watch a funny
movie. Neither one did much for his mood.

I feel a little dizzy, put my head down. This is a dead giveaway.

"Anna, are you okay?"

"Mostly."

I know I don't seem all that strong right now, but I am strong!

I get things done. I don't give up.

I sit up. "I'm fine now."

She puts her hand over her heart. I open my Actor's Journal. It's got my notes on the roles I've played and how I got ready for them.

Okay, I'm an oak tree. . . .

It's a non-speaking part that doesn't showcase my talent, but that means I act entirely with my face.

A tree has confidence, right?

I've got to let my roots go down deep.

When an actor goes the extra mile, that's when the magic happens.

Now suddenly, the breeze seems sweeter, everything seems better.

We're on a winding tree-lined road, and here come

the flowers. Everywhere. They hang from streetlights, they tumble over fences—pink ones, blue ones, yellow, white, red, orange. Mom drives past a hand-painted sign for the Rosemont Flower Festival.

BIGGER THAN EVER!
BETTER THAN EVER!

I wonder if I'll still be here for the festival.

I can smell the flowers' perfume. Mom drives by fences covered with wild roses. Two brown bunnies watch our car go by. I wave at them.

"It seems like nothing bad could ever happen here, Mom."

"Nothing bad is allowed to happen. It's the unofficial town motto."

Mom drives by another sign, much bigger:

CRUDUP'S COUNTRY MARKETS
YOU CAN ALWAYS DEPEND ON US!

There's a picture of a man smiling much too wide.

We drive past the Rosemont Stables. A few horses are in the field. I love horses.

Mom turns onto Flower Road, Mim's street.

Every house has stone steps leading to the front, every house has flowering trees and gardens bursting with color.

Then there's Mim's house. . . .

A painted blue fence, a porch swing, a crazy parrot figure by the front door. A purple banner flaps in the breeze. A trellis is covered with flowers. Warm light shines everywhere.

Mim is a florist. Actually, she's more than that.

She's got the ultimate green thumb. She's got a florist shop in town, but she's really a flower designer.

Actually, she's more than that.

And now I see bubbles rising in the air just above the rosebush in her front yard. They float up near the magnolia tree, carried on the breeze.

I twirl around laughing as they fly overhead.

"Well." Mom laughs. "Your grandmother has outdone herself."

Believe me, that's really saying something.

Four

"It makes five hundred bubbles a minute. Aggie's grandson finally got off his butt and rigged it up."

Mim walks toward us. And you have to understand what happens to my grandmother's face when she sees me; it's like the sun shines through her. I stand in the perfect warmness of that and give her a long hug.

"All right now, Anna, let me look at you. . . ."

I spin around as bubbles land on my face.

"You're looking fine, girl."

"You are too, Mim." She's wearing her growing clothes—dirty jeans, dirty boots, and her big blue-and-white checked shirt with the sleeves rolled up. Her eyes are royal blue; they don't miss much.

She puts her arm around Mom. "How are you, honey? You've had a time."

Mom bites her lip, squares her shoulders.

Excuse me, but I've had a time, too!

We walk past Mim's white pickup truck with FLOWER PEOPLE written in curly purple letters. We head up the steps to her green front door, which is always open. Nobody locks their doors here except the sheriff.

Her old dog, Bean, comes up wagging his tail. I drop my bags, kneel down, and rub him till my hands get tired; he rolls on his back so I can get his stomach. "Okay, that's enough for now." Bean looks hopefully at Mom.

Mim shakes her head. "It's never enough with this dog. I'm trying to teach him contentment, but he lives for the moment, won't take the long view."

We walk in, past a bright purple wall with a sign: NO WHINING.

Piles of books are everywhere. There's a red Chinese chest next to a yellow rocking chair, a fluffy green rug, and above the fireplace in a silver frame:

GO FORTH AND SET THE WORLD ON FIRE

That's what I want to do!

I flop into the hugging chair and pull the fluffy arms of the chair over my shoulders. It's big, deep, and soft. There's something almost human about this chair. Next to a painting of sunflowers that Mim painted is a picture of me and my parents smiling. Mom and Dad had just had a big fight right before that was taken.

You can't always trust a photograph.

But you can trust a hugging chair. I close my eyes and feel about six, the best kind of six, when you're young enough to jump into a lap and get a bear hug and be covered with a blanket and know, just know, that everything is going to be all right.

I open my eyes and see Mom standing there. I look at her, really look, the way Mr. Dez taught us to see things as actors.

Going past her deep brown eyes.

Her sunburned nose.

Her feather earrings.

Her bright green shirt, her white jeans.

So, if I was my mom right now . . . how would I be feeling?

I'd be scared at what's happening to the marriage.

I'd be grateful Mim is here so Anna can be in a safe place.

I'd be worried about the future, angry at my husband, and so not looking forward to living with Barry, his wife Pru, and all those eggs.

I'd be wondering about everything.

I'd be trying to seem brave.

I get up from the hugging chair and beam a mega smile at Mom.

"I'm okay," I tell her.

Basically, this is true.

She studies my face.

I raise one eyebrow, wiggle my ears. *You doubt me?*

She laughs, wipes the tears away.

"Brownies?" Mim calls from the kitchen.

You need to understand the power of these brownies. Dad says if astrophysicists discovered this force, life as we know it would change.

"Maybe just one," Mom says.

Ha!

Mim comes out of the kitchen with a tray of brownies. A tear rolls down my mother's face. "I'm sorry. I didn't come here to cry. . . ."

Maybe you did, Mom.

✿　✿　✿

Mom and Mim are in the garden talking, sitting in the deep blue chairs under the arbor covered with grape vines. But I'm in an even better place: on the roof deck of Mim's house. It fits into the flat part of the roof; there's a ladder leading up and a thin white railing. There are big outdoor pillows up here. I'm on one of them, eating blue-ribbon brownies. My grandpa Mel built this deck. It's the best place to quiet your heart.

I look across from the roses by the split-rail fence to the rich, green grass. The sprinkler is busy watering; the sunshine is better here than anywhere. I look out past Mim's fence to the next house over—Dr. Gudrey's house. It sits up on a hill surrounded by trees. A yellow butterfly flits by.

Mom and Mim look like they're talking about something superserious. I wonder if they're talking about me. I wave, but they don't see. It's so quiet, not like Philadelphia. My grandpa came up here to think; he said it gave him a higher perspective. Grandpa Mel was a roofer, and he always looked at things from the top down.

"On the roof," he'd tell me, "you see things differently. When you can get on top of a problem, you can begin to patch up the holes and the leaks that you couldn't see before."

When Dad wondered if he should go back to school and get his teaching degree, he came up here to think about it. Everything seemed to say yes, so he did and he taught seventh grade math for five years.

Then the school had to make budget cuts . . .

The brand-new teachers were let go . . .

And then Dad was laid off . . .

He changed after that.

He had to go back to being an accountant, which he hated.

He had to leave the thing he loved, the thing he'd worked so hard to achieve.

I wish my dad and I could sit here again like we used to.

And now I see a horse—it's far away, but it looks white with a black mane. There's a rider on it. The horse is racing across the hills, and it's like that person and horse are one great thing of speed.

I've been on a horse exactly twice. The first time went well, the second time I got thrown and sprained both wrists.

Mom said, "No more lessons."

"Mom, that's breaking the rules. When you fall off a horse, you've got to get right back on!"

"No," she said.

I love horses.

The sprinkler stops; the water droplets gleam in the light.

My phone pings. It's Lorenzo—he loves horses, too, as long as they're not moving. He gets extreme motion sickness.

His message: This week's challenge: Do three things you've never done before. Are you in?

I smile, type: Yes.

Our friend Becca, who is away for the summer, too, writes: Already done 4 things today I've never done before. I hate this camp.

Lorenzo: But have you done this?

I click on a photo of Lorenzo clinging to a horse on a moving carousel looking like he's going to lose his lunch: Stayed on for 2 min/didn't puke.

Me: Awesome!!!!!

Mom calls from the garden. "Anna, I have to go."

I feel a pang in my heart as I pocket my phone and climb down the ladder.

I wish she could stay longer.

She and I fold our arms the exact same way and look at each other. "We can do this, Mom."

She smiles. "Yes, we can. And I expect great reports from you."

I laugh. "Anna in Flowerland."

I walk her out to the car, give her an intensely long hug. "Major bravery, Mom. That's what we're going for here."

She salutes, gets in the car. "I love you."

"I love you, too."

And she's off.

And here I am, holding tight to major bravery.

It's only a separation, I tell myself.

I picture my parents separating, like pan juices and fat do in a gravy separator. The fat comes to the top, the juices stay at the bottom.

We did a science video of this in school. I was a water droplet, Lorenzo was a hunk of fat. We had a fight because fat and water don't mix—Lorenzo went one way and I went the other. We got six hundred and eighty-one hits on our video, mostly from me and Lorenzo checking to see if anyone was watching it.

Mim walks out. "This week," I tell her, "I need to do three things I've never done before."

She laughs. "That won't be a problem."

Five

I wake up early. Bean is licking my toe. Peanut never does this. I giggle.

From the kitchen Mim says, "I think he's bored."

Bean gets his disgustingly gross tennis ball that he's been chomping on for years and presses it into my hand.

"I have to go to the bathroom, and then we'll play."

Bean makes a disappointed noise.

"It's not like I go outside, lift my leg, and it's over."

Another noise.

"Deal with it."

✿ ✿ ✿

Mim hands me a warm strawberry muffin as Bean and I head outside. Can I tell you how good this muffin tastes? Strawberries and brown sugar swirls are in every bite.

✿ ✿ ✿

Bean is getting impatient. We walk down the path that circles Mim's garden. The daylilies are awake and open to the sun, the peonies are fat and pink, with ants crawling all over them. Baskets hang on the trellis that my grandpa Mel put up right before he died. Butterflies dance around Mim's daisies. She even has a mirror behind a tree that makes the flowers near the back door feel like they're right in front of you.

Bean whines.

"We're getting there. You can't rush in a magical place."

We head down the stone path past the wisteria vines. We get to the clearing by the split-rail fence. Bean drops the ball and looks at me.

"How lucky do you feel today?" I ask him.

He wags his tail, I pick the ball up and throw it high. Bean jumps up and catches it in his mouth. This is his big talent. I throw it again—he catches it running, like a baseball player going for a pop fly. He rolls it back to me. I throw a grounder to the fence. He gets that one, too. He rolls it back to me.

There's a noise behind me.

"Whoa, Zoe."

I turn to look.

A white horse with a black mane and black legs is standing there. A girl older than I am sits in the saddle. They come right up to the fence. She's got deep-green eyes and the longest eyelashes. I think this is the horse I saw when I was sitting on the roof deck.

"Don't come at her from the front," the girl says. "She'll spook."

I step to the side and look at this horse's head, the small pattern of black splotches on the neck. I want to touch her.

"Our grandmothers are friends," the girl says to me. She points behind her to the house on the hill. Dr. Gudrey lives there. "I'm Taylor."

"I'm Anna."

Taylor nods like she knows that. She pats the horse's neck. "This is Zoe."

I wave at the horse. "Hi."

Taylor reaches down and hands me a piece of an apple. "Give it to her, but from the side."

I do this. Zoe takes the apple from my hand.

I breathe out slow.

"You can rub her shoulder a little."

I climb up on a split rail of the fence and rub Zoe's shoulder. I haven't been close to a horse in a long time. "Good girl, Zoe," I say. I remember being thrown. Zoe looks at me. Her eyes are so soft. I look down.

I've got some issues, okay?

But I keep rubbing. "How you doing, Zoe? Does this feel good?"

And now this horse brings her head close to me and puts it near my shoulder. I figure if this wasn't okay, Taylor would say something.

I stand here and don't move.

"How long are you here for?" Taylor asks.

"I don't know."

Taylor nods like she knows what that's like.

Zoe nuzzles me. I didn't know horses do this.

"Do you ride?" Taylor asks.

"No."

"You should ride," she says. "There's nothing like it."

Taylor makes a quiet noise and Zoe turns from the fence; a quick touch of the reins and Zoe starts trotting . . .

Then goes faster . . .

Taylor rides this horse like it's the easiest thing in the world.

I can't tell you how much I want to do that.

"That girl on the horse . . ." I say to Mim as she and I climb into the pickup.

"You met Taylor. Good. . . ." Mim backs out of the driveway. "She's one resilient kid. I do believe it was the horse that saved her."

"Zoe?"

I wait for Mim to tell me the story, but she doesn't. She drives down the street and turns left by a painted unicorn.

I laugh. "I love that!"

"We have a lot of those around. Some towns paint cows, we paint unicorns."

Past a gazebo now, past a park with a sign, CRUDUP GARDENS, past more unicorns, another huge road sign:

CRUDUP'S COUNTRY MARKETS
YOU CAN ALWAYS DEPEND ON US!

Mim pulls into the back of Flower People, her shop, the best place for flowers anywhere. "Anna, my girl, are you ready to touch lives?"

I laugh. "Always."

Mim throws a crazy purple scarf over her shoulders. "That's the right answer."

❀ ❀ ❀

Mim's in action, doing a dozen things at once.

A guy, maybe sixteen, comes in holding mum plants. "The funeral procession starts at noon."

Mim nods and puts two bouquets together. "Get me the mint and the catnip."

What?

The guy hands these to her, and she puts them in the bouquets.

"Anna, say hello to Burke."

"Hello to Burke," I say.

The guy smiles. "You're the actor."

I shake my hair dramatically. "Yes."

Burke looks at his list, looks at Mim. "Cassidy's needs as many dogwoods as we've got, Mirando's now only wants pink roses for the wedding . . ."

"They need to stop changing their mind." Mim groans.

"And," Burke continues, "Carl Bristol called and wants to know if he can water his cactus with coffee."

"What kind of coffee?"

Burke looks at his paper. "French roast."

"Tell him once a month, no more. Anna, Burke here can put up an arbor one-handed. My kind of man."

Burke smiles. He's got light blond hair and an almost-beard. He's wearing jeans, sandals, and a green Flower People T-shirt.

I'm standing by the indoor fountain looking at the pots and baskets hanging from the ceiling. Mim points at me.

"Girl, you've got big deliveries to make today."

"I do?"

"They require a person of your unique gifts."

Burke laughs in a way that makes me nervous.

✿ ✿ ✿

I ring the doorbell at Leona Cushman's house with my elbow because the vase of roses I'm holding is so big—it's an "I'm Sorry" bouquet sent to her from her husband, Harold.

I don't know what Harold did, but Mim said it's my job to sell the apology.

A lady opens the door. "Mrs. Cushman?" I ask.

"Yes . . ." She looks at the flowers and smiles.

Flowers aren't all she gets this morning.

I hand them to her, take a big gulp of courage.

You can do this, Anna.

My mouth feels dry, but I need to get over that.

"Woo woo..." I sing.

Now I start swaying.

He's sorry.
Woo woo woo.
Really sorry.
Uh-oh!
Let the flowers show how much he cares.
Woo woo woo.
He's sorry!
Woo woo...

I go for the big finish, throw my hands out . . .

Wooooooo!

My voice cracks on the high note. I hate when that happens.

I wrote this little song in the car. If Lorenzo was here, we'd have harmony. It's so much easier to sing with somebody else.

Mrs. Cushman gives me a big tip and shouts, "You've outdone yourself, Mim!"

Mim waves from the truck, and we're off to, I'm not kidding, the pet cemetery.

"No singing on the next one," Mim warns. "Look solemn even though you're a dog person."

"Meow."

One down on Things We've Never Done Before.

❀   ❀   ❀

I carry two bouquets past the headstones:

BIG MONGREL

FUR E. BALL

MISS BITSY

There's a small group of old ladies gathered in a circle. Mrs. Bernstein comes forward, crying. I hand her the bouquet with fresh mint and catnip, her cat's favorite things.

"I'm sorry for your tragic loss, ma'am."

Mrs. Bernstein sniffs. "I believe Empress is happier up there."

An old lady calls, "God knows she wasn't happy down here!"

I nod meaningfully and leave. Two down on the Things We've Never Done Before challenge. I walk toward the pickup. A tall woman is talking to Mim.

"If you must know, Mim, it's the Tourism Council. They're concerned."

"You're the head of that council, Doria."

This woman goes into all-out snark: "How long have we known each other?"

Mim smiles like it's been too long.

"And in that time, have I ever asked you to do something that wasn't for the benefit of the town?"

Mim keeps smiling.

"Coleman Crudup is protesting his placement in the parade, Mim. He gives so much money to this event, and he feels strongly that last year his float should have won a trophy."

Mim leans against her truck. "Last year he cheated, Doria. His float design was taken from one in the Rose Bowl Parade. The designs have to be original. You know that."

This tall lady isn't happy. "Mim, Coleman Crudup is a major force in this town. We need to keep him happy."

Mim adjusts her purple scarf. "I believe in taking care of everyone in town, and those who respect the rules should get precedence at the festival over those who don't."

I think Mim needs some help, so I walk up. The

tall lady looks at me, not impressed. "You're the grand-daughter. . . ."

"I'm Anna, ma'am." I smooth my Kids Act Out shirt from the Children's Drama Workshop.

"I hear you're amusing. . . ."

I wiggle my nose. People love this in Philadelphia. This woman stares at me.

"You must show us your full range of talents some-time, dear. I love to be entertained."

I smile. *Really?*

❀   ❀   ❀

Mim is driving down Rose Street: a man hangs twin-kling lights shaped like flowers over Mabel's Cafe, a giant winking sunflower turns on top of Crudup's Country Market, Star Nails is offering 20 percent off on all flower nail designs from now until the festival. I look at my nails, which I've chewed to stubs.

"Everything is bigger than I remember, Mim."

I haven't been here for the festival in years—I was always at the Children's Drama Workshop summer program.

"And you won't believe the crowds that show up. We spent a lot of time in Rosemont trying to figure out what's the best gift we've got to offer that might bring in some tourism. We always had fine gardens, so we built from there, and now"—she laughs—"we've created a monster."

She turns down a winding road lined with bushes shaped like animals.

"Who did those, Mim?"

"Burke."

"You're kidding!" I look at a bird, a dog . . .

"That boy's got deep rivers." Mim pulls into the parking lot of the Rosemont Library. We get out of the truck, walk past a bush shaped like a camel and up the steps. "You'll hear a lot more about this while you're here, Anna, but I want to maintain the heart of this town and this festival. Not grow it too big, to where we can't handle things. But some people keep pushing for more. . . ."

"Like Coleman Crudup?"

Mim stops for a second and looks so tired. "He's the richest man in town, and he expects to get his way."

Six

"I hear you were a cranberry."

The boy is wearing a T-shirt that reads POSSIBLE GENIUS, and he is holding a weird pink hat with petals.

I look at the hat. "Four shows a day on the weekends. I had a nine-week run."

He twirls the hat. "Winnie Dugan asked me to talk to you. She's in an extra-long meeting with people who drive her crazy." Mim's in that meeting. Winnie is one of the librarians here and Mim's best friend.

The boy holds up two costumes. Both look lame. "We're trying to get kids to help get out the word about the festival, and Winnie wondered if you'd like to be a flower and pass out information."

A kid dressed like a sunflower walks by, not doing much with the role.

"Daisy or petunia?" the possible genius asks.

As a professional, I need hard facts to make this

choice. I take out my phone, look up daisies and petunias.

Points for daisies: simple beauty, popularity. Daisies cheer people up.

Points for petunias: toughness, they keep blooming in cold weather. You can count on a petunia.

That settles it. "Petunia," I tell him.

He hands me the pink costume with the weird petal hat and points to the bathroom. "You can change in there, Petunia."

"My name's Anna. We're doing this now?"

"You have something better to do?"

Guess not . . .

I look at him. He's got dark glasses and dark straight hair that falls in his face. "Do you have a name other than Possible Genius?"

"You can just call me Genius."

"What does your mother call you?"

"Difficult."

❀ ❀ ❀

I would like to say that this puffy pink outfit was not well thought out.

It bounces when I move.

The hat is shaped like an upside-down trumpet, and the petals fall in my face.

I look at myself in the mirror of this one-person bathroom.

I do not look like a tough flower, okay?

My mind goes round and round like a hamster on its wheel.

What if . . .

My life is going to change and there's nothing I can do about it?

My parents don't love each other anymore?

My parents need me and I'm not there to help them work things out?

Peanut can't cope and isn't eating?

Lorenzo finds a new acting partner?

A petal from the weird hat flops over my eye.

Blow it back, Anna. You're a petunia.

I do this.

More force, Anna.

I lean toward the mirror.

Look, when the other flowers give up, I'm still blooming.

I laugh at freezing weather.

"Watch me, world, I'm a petunia."

It's official. I'm now three down on the Things We've Never Done Before challenge.

I open the bathroom door, march into the busy library.

A girl asks, "What kind of flower are you?"

"The toughest one in the garden."

"Cool."

I twirl—I think that's appropriate—and walk to the front door. The genius says, "Nice hat."

"The flower festival is in eighteen days," I remind people. I dance around at this news. "We are going to party." I do my break-dance move.

A little moonwalk moment now, walking like I'm moving against gravity—Lorenzo and I practiced this for one entire year.

A man wants to know where the four-day books are. I point.

A woman wants to know if she can return her past-due books to me. "You need a librarian for that, ma'am." I shake one of my leaves toward the information desk.

I do the slide, the funky chicken. I'm not used to working solo—I keep expecting Lorenzo to show up and dance with me. A boy does the funky chicken with some excellent wing action, but it's not the same.

Six men wearing shirts with cactuses on them march in.

The tall snarky lady I saw at the pet cemetery follows them. "Gentlemen, all I'm asking is that your float bring up the rear."

One faces her. "You want us to be last, Doria. You want us to give up our number one position for Coleman Crudup? We're cactuses, not pansies."

Her face gets flushed.

"Tell Crudup to stop pushing the little guys around, Doria."

They march past me. This Doria woman stares at my outfit.

"Hello, ma'am, we met at the—"

She marches past me, too.

Now a group of kids about my age come in. Their shirts say ROSEMONT MIDDLE SCHOOL JAZZ BAND.

I bounce from side to side, say, "All rigghhhht . . . the band is here . . ."

All of them grin except for one pretty blonde girl who is taller than the rest. She walks up to me.

"Who are you?" she demands.

"Ease up, Caitlin," a boy says.

"Who are you?" she says, like I didn't hear the first time.

"Anna McConnell. Who are you?"

She looks shocked, like I'm supposed to know. Hands on her hips. "I'm Caitlin Crudup!"

Hands on my hips, or my stem, actually. "Welcome to the library."

She marches past me. The band goes to talk to the genius.

Now more people are coming into the library. I've got a good crowd. That always gives me energy. I'm feeling strong, I'm touching hearts, but it's hot in this suit.

The genius walks over. "Okay, that was good. You're hired—for no money."

I smile. *Welcome to community theater.*

"We need you back tomorrow morning, starting at ten. Okay?"

"Okay."

"And, look, that girl Caitlin, she's like that. She's the lead trumpet player." He whispers the next part. "Her dad owns half the town. Don't worry about it."

I nod.

He smiles. "I'm Ben. I'm on drums."

The band walks by. Caitlin glares at me like I'm crawling with bugs.

If I were dressed like a daisy I'd probably keep my mouth shut, but I'm not. I push the pink petals out of my eyes. "Caitlin, if you knew me and decided you didn't like me, that would be okay. But you don't know me. I just got to town, so give it a break."

Her face turns cranberry red.

The band loves that.

Caitlin storms off.

Ben laughs the hardest. "Nice one, Petunia."

I wonder what happens when you insult the spoiled-brat daughter of the richest man in town.

Seven

Mim left her meeting and sent Burke to pick me up.

I have a feeling I made a mistake with Caitlin—she doesn't seem like the kind of girl who lets things go. I lean back in the passenger seat of the Flower People truck. "So, Burke, I keep hearing about this guy, Coleman Crudup."

His face gets tight. "You'll hear more, I'm sure."

"You know him?"

"Yeah . . ."

I drum my fingers on the door. "So, what's he like?"

Burke points a finger at me. "Stay away, Anna. He's not a good guy."

I bite my lip. "Why do you say that?"

"Because I do." He drives up a winding road that gets narrower. "And it just so happens . . ."

Now a huge house appears—it's yellow with white shutters, three stories tall with a wraparound porch filled with plants and wicker furniture. The front door looks like it's built for a giant. There are balconies by the windows and three chimneys on the roof.

Burke pulls up by the locked gate. "That's one of Crudup's houses."

"How many does he have?"

"A few around here, and at least one on an island somewhere."

"Wow. He's rich."

"Money-wise he's rich, but not in any other way."

I nod. I get the difference. "I met his daughter. She doesn't like me."

Burke smiles. "I'd take that as a compliment." He backs the truck up. "Come on, I want to show you something else."

❖   ❖   ❖

It's long and gray, at least a block long, and it doesn't have windows. The roof is rounded and trucks are parked outside.

"It used to be an old airline hangar," Burke explains, "but now . . ."

We go through the huge doors.

Oh, wow!

This is where the floats are being decorated for the parade.

"In a week we'll have so many volunteers, you won't be able to move in here."

There's scaffolding everywhere—a few people are high up on it, decorating, painting.

Burke points to a float in the corner. "That's for the library. They're going to have a twenty-foot bookworm covered in flowers."

Fun!

"And over there is the middle school jazz band float."

It's not as big as the others, but still. I walk with Burke past all the floats. There's yellow caution tape around some of the areas. A lady climbs up a ladder and waves at Burke.

"The flowers go on the last few days," he explains. "If we put them on too early—they'll die." He touches the float we're passing. It says CACTUS CHARACTERS on the side with prickles coming out of the sign.

"They just grow cactuses," Burke explains. "No flowers."

A man working on that float raises a paintbrush. "Cactuses have flowers, boy."

"You're right, sir."

"We've got four hundred and sixty-three of them showing up."

Burke grins. "That's going to be great, Mr. Burley." He tells me, "You won't even recognize these floats by parade time. People work day and night."

"Where's Coleman Crudup's float?"

Mr. Burley says, "Crudup thinks he's above it all. He doesn't want people to see his design till the parade."

Burke looks up at the scaffolding. "Crudup doesn't get it, Anna. When my family first moved to town, I volunteered as one of the decorators. It's hard to explain what happens. People come from all over to help decorate the floats. They don't get paid, but they get to be part of something special that gives a lot of people happiness."

I look at the middle school jazz band float. There's a big note on a musical staff rising above the stage. The words above it say MIDDLE SCHOOL BLUES. That's cool. I want to work on that one.

I bet Caitlin will have a few words to say about that.

Maybe it was the petunia thing or what I said or didn't say, or maybe she doesn't like medium-height girls with curly hair, or maybe she's just a major-league mean girl that I should avoid like food poisoning.

Dad told me if he didn't respect someone, he didn't care if they liked him or not.

I want people to like me. Actors need this.

So, if I were Caitlin Crudup, what would I be about?

I shake that thought from my head. I don't want to think about Caitlin. But it doesn't want to leave.

If I were Caitlin Crudup . . .

I'd be used to getting my own way.

I'd want to always be in charge.

I'd probably know that not everyone likes my father. Lots of people don't, probably.

I know what that's like—just a little.

And then this thought comes . . .

If I were Caitlin Crudup, maybe I wouldn't even like my father.

Or maybe she's exactly like him.

That's probably it.

I don't like the way my dad is acting these days, but I know what he can be, and I'm not giving up on that.

I don't know what to do about it, but I'm not giving up.

❀ ❀ ❀

We're heading back to Mim's. Burke stops the pickup at a stop sign on a narrow road.

"Oh!" I say.

Out from behind the trees walks Zoe with Taylor in the saddle. Taylor waves at us. Burke gets out, grinning.

"Hi," he says to her, still grinning.

"Hi." She looks down. This girl is so pretty, but not as pretty as this horse.

I can't stay in the truck. Zoe and I are connected. I walk slowly toward Zoe, not paying attention to anything else.

"Hi, girl," I say.

Zoe swishes her black tail. "Take a couple steps back," Taylor tells me. "It shows respect. Let her invite you in."

I do this. Zoe turns her head toward me. I look at Taylor.

"Be specific in what you tell her, Anna."

"Okay. Zoe, I'm going to walk up to your side now and pat you."

Zoe looks at me with the softest eyes.

"We're already friends," I remind her. "All right, I'm walking now." I do this slowly. "That's a girl." I put my hand on her side. "I'm going to rub you." And I do this. "Does that feel good?"

Zoe cocks her head at me.

"You're going great," Taylor says. "Nice and easy. She

was shot by a hunter. It was an accident, but she was really skittish for a while. I worked with her for a year."

I can't stop patting this horse. "She's so beautiful."

Taylor looks down. "Anna, here's what you need to know about a horse. They're just like us. They know when you love them."

That's the coolest thought.

Taylor gives me an apple. I hold my hand out, and Zoe takes it. And I don't know why, but I just feel the mess with my dad right now. Zoe shakes her head, flares her nostrils, and backs up.

I back up, too.

I look at Taylor. "What happened?"

"I don't know, she picks up on moods."

I stand there trying to not be moody.

"You've had your Z moment. Don't worry, you'll have more." Taylor makes a clicking sound, and she and Zoe walk across the road and trot up the path on the hill.

Burke stands there watching, smiling.

He stands there longer than is necessary, in my opinion.

A car comes up behind us and starts honking.

Burke jumps into the pickup. I get in, too.

I take out my phone and send this to Lorenzo and Becca: I've had my Z moment.

Lorenzo writes back: Zorro?

Better than Zorro.

Becca: You went to a zoo?

No cages here—everything is free! I miss you guys.

Lorenzo writes: Good!!

✿   ✿   ✿

I look at the plastic rhino on Mim's bookcase. It's got teeth marks on it—from Bean, probably.

"Rhino, I used to play with you. Do you remember?"

I inhale through my nose, throw my voice. "I remember," I make it say.

"Life was simpler then," I tell the rhino.

Another nose inhale. "Tell me about it."

When you can throw your voice, you're never really alone.

But I could sure use a friend in this town.

I put the rhino down, stand in front of the full-size mirror, cock my head, make a rubber face.

I raise one eyebrow, put it down.

I push back my hair and wiggle my ears. I'm rusty at this.

I get close up to the mirror and wiggle my nose. This is close to my best trick.

I stand on one leg, then the other.

Mr. Dez always told us, "The world doesn't need more cookie cutter people!"

I stand there looking.

I go deeper.

I see a girl whose dad needs to sit on his anger and he can't.

I see a girl who wants to be home and wants to be here at the exact same time.

I flop into the hugging chair and try not to think about my life.

Mim comes in. "Are you singing much these days?"

"Not really."

"Winnie said that the girl who was singing with the middle school jazz band has to have her tonsils out. The band needs a singer." Mim looks at me.

I go deeper into this chair.

"And, not that it's my place to volunteer you . . ." Mim says.

"You always volunteer me!"

"So I'm staying in character, but I did mention that you can sing."

"I don't really sing!"

"You sang when you delivered the "I'm Sorry" bouquet. And I distinctly remember you as a singing radish. You got a standing ovation."

That was one of my best moments ever.

"Winnie said she'd let them know."

"Mim!"

"How can it hurt to let them know?"

Caitlin Crudup jumps to mind. She doesn't want me anywhere near her.

Mim's phone rings. She walks out of the room saying, "Doria, Coleman Crudup's placement in the parade is number seven, also known as last. And, no, he cannot pay for his daughter to lead the parade. This parade is not for sale!"

✿ ✿ ✿

Morning. Eight twenty. I'm warming up my voice.

Ah ah ah ahhhhhhhh ah ah ahhhhhhhhhh

I go up one note.

Ah ah ah ahhhhhhh ah ah ahhhhhhhhhhh

Bean is in the bathroom holding his disgusting, mangy ball.

"What?"

Bean drops the ball. It rolls toward me.

"I have to get ready. I have to be a petunia."

I put pink blush all over my face, pink lipstick. I put on mascara. Petunias need long lashes. I flutter my lashes.

Don't mess with me.

Bean whines.

"I can't play with you in this outfit."

Ah ah ah ahhhhhhhhhhh ah ah ahhhhhhhhhh

Honestly, I'm up to being a petunia. Not much else.

Definitely not a singer.

My phone rings. It's Mom.

"Hi."

"Well, hi." She sounds like she's trying to hold it together.

"Have you broken any eggs?"

That's a joke. She doesn't get it. "Oh, Anna, how are you?"

Mom, you sound awful.

"I've sort of got a job." I mention the petunia.

She half laughs. "You've got range, honey."

"Mom, you don't sound too good."

"Well, I've been better."

Bean pushes his ball to me. I kick it back. He pushes it again.

"Do you have time to talk, Anna?"

"I'm supposed to be at the library, I can call and say I'll be—"

"No, we'll talk later."

"Mom, did something happen?"

She's quiet.

"Dad's okay?" I say this louder.

"Yes. We'll talk later. I love you."

Call ended.

But not really.

My mind seems to be finishing all the sentences.

She and Dad had an awful fight.

They're going to get a divorce.

She wants me to come home.

I suppose I could do that. I can hang out with Lorenzo.

They're selling the house.

Peanut died.

No, she would have told me right then.

She's got some terrible disease . . . or Dad does . . . or I do.

Stop it, Anna.

Eight

"I hear you're a singer," Ben says.

I shake my head. Petals fall in my face.

"Winnie told me. Librarians don't lie."

"I sing like anybody else."

I try hard to look like I mean it, but it's hard to look serious in a puffy petunia suit. I head toward the front of the library.

I'm not going to go round and round about my call with my mother.

No hamster brain allowed. The show must go on!

"We need a singer in the band," Ben says after me.

Run it by Caitlin first, okay?

I pull down in my actor's soul. Today I'm going deep as a petunia.

The library doors open. Three little kids run in and instantly hug me.

"Hey," I shout, "this is the way to start the day!"

We start dancing, and their mothers are smiling. More kids show up, more parents—in just a few minutes I've got a crowd.

People take my picture.

Puffy pose.

A little girl comes up to me and whispers, "I didn't want to come to the library, because my best friend said she hates me."

"That's hard. I'm glad you came."

She goes to the children's section, gets a book, and comes back to read it here.

When you hurt you need people around you.

"Yes, the library float has a bookworm." That's Winnie Dugan walking by on her phone. "It is not a tired symbol, Doria, it's classic. We have a huge book decorated with roses and a reading tree. We'll have one hundred mum plants decorating the staircase."

Winnie looks at me. I wiggle my nose. She smiles. She needed that.

Back to the ever-growing group.

"Petunia, will you read to me?"

"Petunia, will you be my babysitter?"

Three little boys, triplets, start twirling me around. I don't even know how much time has passed, but all of a sudden I feel so tired.

"You guys," Ben shouts, "leave the petunia alone." He points to the children's room. They scurry in there.

Ben hands me an iced tea. "Take a break, Anna."

I take off my petal hat and head outside. My hair is wet from sweating. I sit on the library steps next to the camel-shaped bush.

I look at the camel. "How's it going?"

Voice trick time. "I'm thirsty," it says.

A boy asks me. "How did you do that?"

"It's a secret." I do it again.

A man and woman walk up holding hands; they smile at me.

My parents used to hold hands.

I drink my tea as an old van pulls up. A lady gets out, shouting on her purple phone, smoking a long cigarette. She's not speaking English; she looks Asian. She puts on big white sunglasses.

A man sits in the driver's seat of the van. A girl is in the back looking out the window. I wave to her; she waves back a little. The man honks the horn, and the lady on the phone yells something at him I don't understand. He yells back.

I look at the girl in the van. My parents fight, too.

The girl hits the window. The man shouts. The woman walks over, waves her cigarette at me. She's wearing a hot pink shirt with a silver star.

"You show," she says with a thick accent, "ba room."

"What?"

"Ba room!"

"Bathroom?"

She nods.

"There's one inside."

"You show." The woman shouts to the man, who gets the girl out of the van. The girl is nervous, looking around. The woman throws her cigarette down, grabs the girl's hand, drags her over, then says to me, "Okay, now you show."

"This way."

I put my petal hat back on—it's important to stay in character. I walk them to the bathroom behind the return desk. The girl is looking everywhere, almost like she's never been in a library before. She has the biggest eyes. She looks at my outfit.

"I'm a petunia," I explain.

The lady says something in another language, and instantly the girl looks down.

"This is it," I tell them. "There's only room for one at a—"

The woman goes in with the girl, slams the door shut.

Winnie Dugan is saying to a boy, "Roland, you can't take any more books out. You have eight overdue. . . ."

I hear a flush, and the door opens. The woman leads the girl outside by the arm, back into the van.

I walk back outside to get my iced tea and watch as they drive too fast out of the parking lot and almost crash into an SUV turning in. The van screeches to a stop. The SUV honks and pulls around the back. Then the side door of the van opens.

The girl jumps out and tries to run.

The man jumps out and catches her. "She sick, she sick!"

For a half second she looks pleadingly at me—this girl is scared. The man carries her back to the van and drives off.

What was . . . ?

Did anyone else see this?

I look around. I'm the only one out here.

I run inside. A little girl says, "Wanna dance, flower girl?"

"Not right now."

I run up to Winnie Dugan, who is saying, "I'm sorry to hear about your turtle dying, Roland, but borrowing a book is a sacred trust."

"Did you see that?" I interrupt.

A girl with short brown hair runs out of the bathroom. "Siri," a woman shouts to her, "I swear, if we are late and miss that plane . . . !"

"I'm coming, Mom." The brown-haired girl looks at me strangely. She and her mother head for the door.

I turn to Winnie. "The girl who was in here with that lady . . . who went to the bathroom . . . did you see it?"

"I did. It seemed odd. Who was she?"

"I don't know."

People walk by and smile at my outfit.

I feel dizzy. I grab onto a tall bookcase.

"Something about that child," Winnie mentions. "What kind of car did they have?"

"It was a van."

"What kind?"

"I don't know."

"What color?"

I try to remember. "Blue, maybe? Brown. I'm not sure." I mention the lady's hot pink shirt. "There was a star on it."

"I didn't notice that."

I'm remembering when Becca's cousin Martin tried to jump out of a car; her uncle had to carry him back inside and give him his medicine.

Maybe this was the same thing.

Or not.

And if not . . .

"I think the girl might be in trouble, Winnie."

"I wasn't paying attention when they first came in, but as they were leaving . . ."

Winnie asks the other librarian if she saw anything. She didn't.

I run outside to get air. I stand on the library steps gulping it in.

My heart's beating so fast.

What just happened?

I sit on the steps, put my head between my legs, and try to slow my breathing down.

I'm trying to remember everything I saw.

The girl.

Her huge eyes.

The scratched van.

They were Asian. The girl and the lady. I think the man was, too.

I know this much—I'd better remember.

I'd better get it right.

Nine

I'm sitting at a picnic table behind the library. Ivy crawls over the wooden fence. Mim is here, Winnie, and Ben.

I say, "How do you know if you really saw something or you just think you did?"

Mim says, "Sometimes you don't know the difference."

"Then what do you do?"

"You test it." That's Winnie.

I tell them every detail I can remember.

"The man driving the car was angry. He had a wide face. He wasn't tall, at least I don't think so . . . I mean, she could just have angry parents or . . . she needs help going to the bathroom. . . ." I shout, "Her hair was brown—dark brown and straight . . . she wore it in a ponytail."

"She was taller than the woman," Winnie mentions.

"That's right! I can't remember what the girl was wearing."

Winnie can't either.

I gulp. "I just remember her eyes—big and wide and sad and brown . . ."

Winnie puts a legal pad in front of me. "Write it down."

"I'm not sure what I saw!"

Ben hands me a pen. "You just went into massive detail, Anna."

"Do it now, honey. Before you forget," Mim adds.

I write:

I was outside when the van pulled into the library parking lot and parked. It was an ugly van, scratched up.

A lady got out, talking on her phone. Another language—not Spanish or French. I know how those sound.

The lady was short.

She was smoking.

The color of her shirt was hot pink.

The picture on her shirt was a star.

The girl in the van had huge, brown eyes and never smiled. I just remember her eyes and how it seemed she wanted to run away.

She tried to run away!

The lady took her by the arm and went into the bathroom with her.

The man driving the car was angry. He had a wide face. He wasn't tall, at least I don't think so.

The girl's hair was brown—dark brown and straight.

She was taller than the woman.

The girl was wearing _____.

The color of the van was _____.

The license plate was _____.

I draw a girl's face with huge eyes, baby animal eyes.

"The girl I saw could just have weird parents or . . . she needed help going to the bathroom . . . or she doesn't need help at all!"

We look at Winnie, who says, "I'm calling the sheriff."

     ❀ ❀ ❀

The sheriff sends Deputy Bitterson, who isn't impressed by what I saw.

"You don't have a name, a license plate, make of car, young lady?"

"It was a van, sir."

"What color?"

I mention the scratches.

"How old was she?"

"Maybe my age. Twelve."

"Deputy," Winnie says, "I saw the girl and the woman, too. This was not a normal situation."

He shakes his head. "There's been no crime that we know of, no report that a girl with this description is missing."

"Do you always need that information?" Winnie demands.

He takes in a breath. "Usually."

I look at the clock on the wall, ticking off the seconds.

How much time is left to find her?

Does she even need to be found?

I look at the deputy. "What if the girl's in trouble?"

He sighs. "Unfortunately, there are lots of kids in trouble."

Does that mean we don't try to help this one?

Winnie mentions getting an artist to draw a composite sketch.

Deputy Bitterson's long face is getting longer. "We

don't have a police sketch artist in Rosemont. Closest one is an hour away."

Winnie leans toward him. "We have a car!"

"Mrs. Dugan, we have a couple thousand people who are going to pour into this town over the next two weeks. We need to make sure we're safe and ready for whatever comes. We don't have the man power to track this down. I'll make out a report."

She's in his face now. "What do you do in emergencies, Deputy?"

"We do the best we can!"

The genius hands him a copy of all I wrote down.

Deputy Bitterson folds it without looking at it.

Then he marches past the four-day book table, turns left at the My Favorite Book shadowbox display, and heads out the door.

✿ ✿ ✿

Mim's backyard is packed to overflowing. There is a patio with a slider chair and a big tree with a rope swing, every branch has a birdhouse painted in bright colors, and a birdbath stands by the hammock; four birds are playing in it as a squirrel watches.

And I can't sit still.

I flop into the slider chair, push it back and forth.

I get up, I sit down.

Mim is grilling bourbon chicken. "Don't talk yourself out of what you saw, Anna."

"I know . . . I'm just confused . . . and worried . . ."

"I can understand both those things. But do not doubt what you saw."

Right.

I'm back in the sliding chair, pushing it back and forth, back and forth, I feel the rhythm of the movement.

I watch the birds splashing. My dad made the big birdhouse. . . . It looks like a bird motel. Several birds fly in and out.

Maybe that girl's mother was just having a bad day.

Back and forth . . .

Mim puts the chicken on a platter. Bean heads over to the grill—he wants this chicken.

"Why shouldn't I doubt what I saw?"

Mim looks right at me with her royal blue eyes. "Because Winnie saw strange behavior, too, and because you're a smart, discerning girl. Live with that. Winnie is checking with someone who knows about these things."

"The sheriff?"

"She has another contact." Mim heads to the table. "Don't overthink it, Anna."

"I can't not think about it!"

"I understand."

"We can't give up!"

"We won't."

If I were a better person, if I'd been paying attention, I would have gotten the license plate and I would have run over there and helped that girl. I could have at least taken a picture with my phone!

Did I do that?

I did not do that!

I sat there

Doing nothing . . .

And now a girl with baby animal eyes might be in serious trouble, and it's all my fault!

Mim carries corn bread to the table, studying my face.

"I'm not overthinking it!"

I grab a piece of corn bread, take a bite.

"This corn bread is amazing."

I sit there trying not to overthink anything, but the

minute you try so hard, every worry you have tumbles out.

I eat some bourbon chicken, and this chicken is beyond great, and I sip my orange juice and I look at Mim and burst into tears.

Mim says, "Come on. I want to show you something . . ."

I shake my head.

I go over what I saw.

The girl's eyes were brown.

Her shirt was—

I bolt up. "She had a yellow scrunchie, Mim! Her hair was in a ponytail! I remember!"

Ten

Blue.

Purple.

White.

Red.

Pink.

Silver.

Where are the yellow ones?

I'm tearing through every scrunchie in the hair section of Debbie's Dollar Daze store.

It's got to be yellow!

I look through the headbands, the combs, and way in the back is a package of three scrunchies, one white, one black, and one yellow.

I hold it up, run to the counter to pay. I see a journal with a white horse on the front, I grab that, too. I can hear Mim leaving a message for Winnie.

Okay, it's not a huge memory, but it's something.

It's another clue!

I pay my two dollars, tell Debbie I don't need a bag, rip the plastic package open, grab the yellow scrunchie, and put it on my wrist like a bracelet, the kind of bracelet people wear when they promise to remember someone who's lost.

I can see her scared eyes when she ran toward me.

I make a fist and raise my hand.

I promise to remember you.

Now more is happening, right here in Debbie's Dollar Daze.

This sweeps into my brain: *The lady in the van had a mole on her chin.*

I buy a silver pen, write that down in my horse journal.

What else?

Her fingernails were painted purple.

And . . .

There's more. I know it . . .

I feel memory so close . . .

But what?

Mim walks over. "You need a break, Anna."

"I can't—"

I'm trying to remember!

I holler, "I need to see the sheriff!"

Debbie at the counter looks nervous. "Is there a problem?"

"Yes," I yell, "and it's huge."

❄   ❄   ❄

The sheriff isn't at the station when we get there. He isn't there the next morning either.

"They're gone for the day." That's what a lady named Maria at the front desk tells me.

"Can't you call them?" I ask.

Mim puts her hand on my shoulder and says to Maria, "Deputy Bitterson filed a report recently on a missing girl . . ."

"Not that I saw." Maria is looking at her computer screen. "This happened when?"

"Two days ago."

Maria shakes her head. "Nothing yet."

How long does it take to file a report?

"He said he'd send the report in," I mention.

"He hasn't done that yet."

"This is an emergency," I add.

"He doesn't seem to think so," Maria says.

I step forward. I know my rights!

At least I think I do.

They might be different when you're twelve, but I've got some.

"Can I give you the information and can you send in the report?"

Maria says, "We don't normally do that."

I'm sick of people talking about normal!

"This is way past normal!" I shout. "And I have more information!"

Mim says, "Maria, please address the seriousness of this."

Maria takes the information about what I saw and where I saw it, and I make sure she types it all in.

"I've got it," Maria says.

"Excuse me, ma'am, but are you going to press send?"

Mim clears her throat.

And Maria sends it.

Mim says, "Okay now, Anna?"

It's not close to okay, but it's a start.

✿ ✿ ✿

That night I sleep with the yellow scrunchie on. I'm not taking it off.

I wake up early with a headache and a stomachache.

Bean is whining that he needs to be let out. I walk

with him through the kitchen, open the back door.

The glow of the early morning is so beautiful. I stand there looking out across Mim's garden. The birds are waking up; the flowers are glistening. I need to get out in this. I slip on my sneakers, grab my horse journal, and head outside in my pajamas.

I walk along the stone path past the birdhouse my father built to the bench by the split-rail fence. I check my messages. I've got five from Lorenzo, three from Becca, three from my mom—everyone asking:

Where are you?

I don't know where I am.

This is supposed to be a vacation.

This is supposed to be a quiet time for me to think.

Bean comes up hopefully with his ball.

"Not now, Bean." But he sits there like he knows what's best.

I need to do something for somebody.

"Just a couple times." I throw the ball. He catches it in midair, brings it back.

I throw it again.

Endlessly.

It's like Bean was made specifically to catch balls.

What was I made especially to do?

I write Lorenzo, tell him what happened.

And I'm here to tell you, only your ultimate best friend, who knows you better than anyone could, would write back and say:

She's lucky it was you who saw her, Anna.
You won't let it go.

Electricity shoots through me.

No, I won't!

I'm going to drive people crazy until they do something to help.

Now my mom calls.

"Anna, I want you to listen. I've thought long and hard about this."

I close my eyes. I already know.

"You're getting divorced, Mom. . . ."

"No. We're working hard to understand what's happened and what to do."

I stand a little straighter. "Okay . . ."

"I think . . . actually, I know that the right thing for you to do now, honey, is to come home so—"

"I can't come home!"

"Anna, I feel that you and I need to come home and your father can stay in Center City with the Dylans. They're such good friends, they said they'd help however they—"

"I can't. Mom! I've got something to do. Something important!"

"What in the world is happening there that is so important?"

I don't know how to tell her. If I tell her, she'll swoop in and get me out of here fast.

"Anna, listen to me. I don't like the way you're sounding. I can hear the stress. I think it's best that we all see Jen individually and as a family so that we can—"

"I don't want to talk to Jen!" I'm shrieking now.

"Anna, I very much want you to feel heard in all this, but sometimes a child doesn't get to decide!"

"Mom, I have to call you back."

"You and I are going to talk this through now, Anna."

"I can't, Mom. I have to think. I love you. Bye."

Did I just hang up on my mother?

Eleven

"Whoa, Zoe . . ."

I turn around and see Taylor sitting on the horse.

My phone is buzzing. It's Mom.

Taylor says, "Do you need to get that?"

Probably, but I can't.

I look at Taylor and start crying.

"I feel like a total idiot. I'm standing here crying in my dog pajamas! I don't know you at all, but you've got to listen to me, Taylor! Listen to everything, okay?"

She jumps off Zoe, ties the reins to the fence. "Okay. Go ahead and tell me, Anna."

I tell her everything about the girl in the van.

And this girl listens with everything she's got.

She doesn't say anything for the longest time, then: "I did a report on missing kids."

I wait.

"What did you learn?"

"I learned it's scary how many are missing, it's awful how people sometimes look the other way, and sometimes there's something that can be done about it. That's what you're doing, Anna. You're doing something."

I don't feel like I'm doing much of anything except sitting in the garden totally stressed out . . .

And then, like a bolt, I remember!

I shout, "I can see it! It was right next to the license plate on the van. An American flag sticker. It was big." I stretch out my hands to almost a foot. "Like this. And . . ." My heart is beating fast as my memory kicks in. "There was a slogan above the flag. 'Proud to be an American,' but the 'can' part of 'American' was torn. I remember!"

I try to draw it in my horse journal, but I'm not that good an artist. Taylor takes the pen from me. "Tell me again. Every detail."

"It was an American flag."

"Straight or flapping?"

"Flapping."

She draws that.

"Not that much flapping."

She draws it again. I nod. "'Proud to be an American' was in square letters."

Taylor draws a *P*. "Like that?"

"Maybe a little bigger."

PROUD TO BE

"That's close."

Taylor keeps trying to get it right. She doesn't exactly, but it's good enough.

I look at Taylor. "Is that enough to find her?"

Taylor takes a deep breath. "I don't know."

"But we can try, right?"

"We're going to kill ourselves trying."

Now Mim walks toward us. Winnie is right behind her. They've got their game faces on.

"Winnie got you an appointment."

"For what?"

Winnie doesn't say.

"It's okay. Taylor knows about the girl. I told her."

Mim nods. "The appointment is to see the police sketch artist."

"When?"

"As soon as we can get there."

I turn to Taylor. "Will you come?"

Taylor nods, climbs over the fence, unties Zoe.

"We'll pick you up in ten," Mim says.

Taylor rides Zoe back to the barn.

Now all I have to do is remember everything perfectly and not mess up.

❀　❀　❀

The artist sits at a table with a drawing pad and pencils in front of her. She smiles at me. "I like your shirt."

It's purple; it says, ACT OUT. I got it at the Children's Drama Workshop. I pull at the shirt, hoping I don't mess up. So much is at stake, it makes my stomach hurt.

"You're visiting, I hear," the artist says to me.

"I'm from Philadelphia."

"Oh, those cheesesteaks . . ."

I nod.

"I'm Daphne. You want to get started?"

"I guess so."

She opens her pad. "Tell me what you saw, Anna."

I tell her about the girl, the woman, the van. Daphne looks at Winnie. "You saw this, too?"

"I didn't see the van, just the woman and the girl."

Mim and Taylor say they're here for emotional support.

I take out the drawing Taylor made of the decal. "This was on the back of the van next to the license plate—on the left."

Daphne studies it. "This is so helpful. Is there anything you want to add or take away from this, Anna?"

Suddenly, I remember something else. "Iowa," I shout.

"What about Iowa?"

"I didn't remember till now. The license plate—it was from Iowa. It said . . ." I try to picture it. "Something about corn."

"'The Corn State'?" Daphne asks. "That's Iowa's license plate slogan."

She draws the back of a van, copies the decal, draws a license plate with THE CORN STATE. "Was it like this?"

My heart is racing. It's hard to think.

"Take your time . . ."

I don't want to make anything up, but, "The van was scratched up."

"Where?"

"In the back, kind of . . ."

"Lots of scratches? Any dents?"

"Lots of scratches on the bumper, I don't know about dents."

Daphne draws scratches. She smudges the pencil with her thumb and looks at me.

I nod.

"What color was the van?"

I shake my head. "I don't remember, but the decal was torn more."

She fixes that.

"That's better."

"You're helping so much, Anna."

I shut my eyes. I've got a headache.

"Tell me the first thing you saw when the van pulled into the library parking lot, Anna."

"I'm not sure if I saw the lady first or the girl. I'm sorry."

"That's okay. You're doing fine. Tell me more about the van. How did it look from the side? Can you remember how many windows it had?"

I gulp. "I can see the girl's face looking out a big window."

"That's good." Daphne shows me some pictures of vans. "Did it look like any of these? Take your time."

I go through page after page and stop at one that has a big, long window like a bus. "It was like that. I can remember the girl looking out of this kind of window."

Daphne draws. "Was she in a small bus, do you think?"

"I . . . I don't know . . . no, it wasn't a bus."

"Like this?" Daphne shows me what she's drawn. Her drawing looks like a bus.

"It wasn't that long or that high, but it had windows like a bus."

She changes the height and the length. "Better?"

"Yes."

She asks questions about the girl. I show her the list I made, tell her about the baby animal eyes.

Daphne draws deep, round, scared eyes on the face of a girl with dark hair.

I mention the ponytail, the scrunchie.

"Let's bring this girl out of the van. What was she wearing?"

I try to think. All I can remember is the lady grabbing the girl's hand. I can see the lady's arm.

I stand up. "She had a tattoo!"

"The girl?"

"The lady!"

Winnie leans back. "I remember that. It was a flower, like a daisy."

"Where?" Daphne holds her pencil, ready.

"Just above the elbow." I look to Winnie. "Right?"

Daphne draws an arm with a daisy tattoo. She draws a stem.

Winnie shakes her head. "No stem."

"The flower was fuller," I mention.

Daphne draws that, but it still isn't right. "What arm? Left or right?"

"Left," I say.

Winnie bites her lip. "It was right, as I remember."

Oh boy.

Daphne smiles. "That's okay. Was the flower like this?"

We help her make it fuller, but how is this going to help find a girl?

Colors are coming to me now.

The lady had a purple phone.

The girl was wearing white sandals.

The man had gray hair that fell over his ears.

The artist shows us pictures of faces. Some are criminals, I figure, some are famous people.

"Was the girl's face round, square, long . . . what do you think, Anna?"

Winnie and I decide it was round.

"And the color of her eyes?"

"Brown." Winnie and I say that together.

"What language did the lady speak?"

"Not Spanish or French. I know what those sound like." Winnie didn't hear them speak.

So much is on me!

Can you remember?

No, not anymore!

I don't want to get it wrong!

"Should we take a break?" Daphne asks.

Yes, please.

✿　✿　✿

Mim hands me and Taylor each a bottle of lemonade that has a picture of a man in an old-fashioned hat smiling like he knows a good secret—the lady he's with is smiling like the world is an easy place.

A police car pulls up—we're standing outside the station—and a big cop gets out. He has two moles on his cheek, his hair is thin on top of his head, he is as tall as my dad, and when he smiles at us he has a space between his two front teeth.

I could go back inside and describe the policeman and the lemonade man and his lady to Daphne and get every detail right.

But it seems the more I think about the girl, the foggier she becomes.

If they can find you, I promise I'll be your friend.

"Memory"—Mim sighs—"is a tricky thing."
"You were amazing in there, Anna." That's Taylor.
I finish my lemonade with a slurp.
"I swear, my brain aches." Winnie rubs her forehead. "How are you, Anna?"
"I wish I could remember more."
"All you can remember is what you can remember."
But is it enough?

❀ ❀ ❀

"We've got a lot here." Daphne shows us the three sketches she's made, of the van, the girl, and the lady with the daisy tattoo. "What do you think? Have we got it?"

This looks real. I felt like part of me is back there at the library. I can feel the anger of the lady, the girl looking at me.

Why didn't I say something then?

Winnie studies the sketches. "This is good, Daphne. Very good. And I've got another piece. The lady had another tattoo on her calf. Her left calf. It was a spider."

I never saw that. I get a chill as Daphne tries to draw a spider.

Spiders weave their webs where no one can see, then they catch their prey.

I close my eyes.

Daphne says, "Like this?"

"Smaller. More sinister."

A spider and a daisy.

Daphne says they will put this out on the wires, and if we think of anything or want to change it, to give her a call. She makes copies of the sketches for us to take home.

We walk outside, get in the car. I'm trying to remember every detail of life. It's a blue Chevy with black seats, and a figure of a woman with children around her is hanging from the rearview mirror. The figure is carved from light-colored wood.

Mim tells me, "When you've done all you can do, rest in that."

Twelve

We stop by Debbie's Dollar Daze to buy more yellow scrunchies. All that Debbie has are the non-important colors.

"The shiny purple ones are nice," she says. "We've got headbands . . ."

"Do you have any more in the back?" Taylor asks.

Debbie doesn't want to go into the back, but I blurt out, "This is life and death! We need yellow scrunchies!"

That gets her moving.

Of course, the last time I was in here, I shouted that I needed to see the sheriff. She looks at me strangely.

Taylor puts her hand on my shoulder. "Anna is just here visiting."

Debbie gives a quick nod, runs into the back.

The number of people in town who don't like me is growing.

But Debbie comes back with three more packages, each with a white, black, and yellow scrunchie.

Winnie, Mim, and Taylor are now wearing them as wrist bracelets.

"You might want to order more," Taylor tells her. "These might catch on."

Mom has left four messages for me. She's talked to Mim and told her in no uncertain terms that she wants me home.

"Anna," Mim says, "try to give your mind a rest if you can. That will help all kinds of things. You can talk to your mother in the morning."

It would be nice if my dad would call. We haven't talked for over a week.

I think of a poem by Robert Frost that Dad had in his classroom. . . . Here's the part I remember:

The woods are lovely, dark and deep,
But I have promises to keep,
And miles to go before I sleep,
And miles to go before I sleep.

Dad didn't just teach math, he taught life.
I write this in my new horse notebook:

To the girl with the baby animal eyes:

Try to look out the window of the van as much as you can, and when you have to go to the bathroom, make sure lots of people see you.

If you get a chance to run away, do it.

You're not invisible anymore, at least part of you isn't.

The police are looking for you, and I'm hoping to remember more so I can help.

I won't forget, I promise.

I won't let it go.

Your friend forever,

Anna McConnell

Okay, now I can sleep.

But just a little.

Thirteen

I walk to the barn. Taylor told me to meet her early.

I'm glad to have something to do, something else to think about.

I touch the yellow scrunchie on my right wrist and wonder how that girl is doing.

I come close to the barn—it's seven in the morning and the light seems to be telling me, slow down, don't worry.

I remember walking into the stable when I had my first riding lesson. I was so excited.

Okay, this is my do-over. Although I'm not mentioning it to my mother.

Taylor is drinking something from a cup with the words I'M A MIRACLE.

I don't feel like a miracle. I never once thought of myself that way.

I get out my phone and send this to Lorenzo and Becca: I'm a miracle.

Taylor doesn't see me yet, but Zoe looks out. And I remember getting thrown like it was yesterday, but I can't focus there.

"Hi, girl," I say.

Taylor smiles. "You look ready."

I nod.

"I just want you to know that the first time I worked with Zoe, she stepped on me. That was the beginning of our relationship."

I back up.

Taylor motions me forward.

"I got thrown once," I mention.

"How old were you when it happened?"

"I was ten. I'm twelve now." I wish I could say I was a more significant age, like fourteen.

She nods. "I was twelve once. Now I'm sixteen."

"So how was it for you—being twelve?"

"Not so good. That's when my mom died."

Nice one, Anna. Open your fat yap and ruin everything. "I'm sorry, I didn't mean to be—"

"It's okay."

No it's not. "I'm sorry you lost your mom."

"It was bad. Everything hurt." She rubs Zoe. "I didn't even want to be thirteen, not without Mom."

Zoe shakes her head. Taylor smiles at me. "I thought my life was over, but all of it got me here. This is a good place to be. Here's the synopsis: my father started dating all these women—he wanted a new wife and he found one."

"Do you like her?"

"No."

I need to stop asking questions.

"I lived with them for two years, nine months, and seventeen days."

Zoe neighs in her stall. "We'll get to you in a minute," she tells the horse. Taylor pushes her straw cowboy hat back. "I asked my dad to send me to boarding school—he said it was too expensive. I got to the right place eventually."

I mention my dad's anger. "That's part of why I'm here," I tell her.

"So we're both tough." Taylor opens the door to Zoe's stall. "Zoe got here three weeks after I did. I think we saved each other. Right, Zoe?"

Zoe gives Taylor a push with her nose. Taylor

laughs. She hands me the reins. "Do you really want to know her?"

"Yes."

"Stretch out your hand, then."

I stretch out my right hand with the yellow scrunchie.

I look at Zoe from the side, I can tell she's waiting. "So, Zoe, this is my hand, my right hand, and I do want to mention that I'm right-handed, so if you were thinking about, say, biting it or eating some of my fingers, that would be bad."

Zoe sniffs my hand.

I look at this white horse with gray and black spots. "I really like you," I say.

Taylor makes a clicking sound. Zoe turns her head. "Get on, Anna."

Uh, this is kind of quick. I like the concept of riding a horse, not—

Zoe shakes her head.

"Maybe she doesn't want me to—"

"Put your foot in the stirrup."

Taylor gives me a lift up. It doesn't take much, and here I am, up on this horse. Up on top of the world. "We're not going fast, right?"

"Not yet." Taylor takes the reins and walks Zoe back

and forth. I like being high, but I tense a little; Zoe shakes her head fast and neighs.

"She can tell you're nervous just now."

"She can?"

Taylor pats her. "It's okay, girl. It's fine."

Zoe backs up and turns around and heads out of the barn. "Uh, this horse is moving. . . ."

Taylor laughs. "Enjoy it!"

I do, sort of, but Zoe keeps going toward the riding ring.

"Pull the reins and say, 'Whoa, girl.'"

I do this, but my voice doesn't sound like I mean it. Zoe seems to be waiting for a strong voice here, because now she's just walking off on her own with me on her back.

"How are you feeling?" Taylor asks.

"Like I might need rescuing. . . ." I remember getting thrown over the fence, landing hard on my hands.

"There's probably lots of things you need, Anna, but I don't think rescuing is one of them."

"Whoa, Zoe." I pull the reins, and instantly she stops. I pat her neck. "Good girl."

Taylor walks over smiling, and suddenly I realize that the whole time I've been with this horse I haven't thought about much of anything else.

Zoe walks with me around and around the ring. I look up. The clouds are moving fast across the sky.

"That's it for today." Taylor helps me down. Zoe stretches her neck and touches my shoulder with her nose.

"That's horse for 'I like you,'" Taylor explains.

I look at Zoe from the side, smile, and say, "I like you, too."

Taylor climbs in the saddle and rubs Zoe's neck. "You okay, Anna?"

I nod. More than okay.

"You did really well." Taylor makes a clicking sound, Zoe turns, and they ride out of the ring into the sunset—actually, it's morning, but you get the idea.

I look at my phone.

From Becca: I'm a miracle, too!

From Lorenzo: What????? You're just figuring out you're a miracle??? I've known this about you for years.

❀   ❀   ❀

I'm walking down the stone path past the birdhouses in Mim's garden. I stop at the bird hotel my father made. It looks like a white frame house with shutters. Birds are flying in and out. Dad is good with his hands.

He's good at so many things, but it's like he left those behind. I don't know why. I think adults can get so super-serious about their careers that they forget that fun is an important part of life. I look at the yellow scrunchie.

I wonder if it's okay to have fun when that girl is out there scared.

I wonder why the world is so different for people.

Here I am safe in this town, but so many kids aren't in a safe place.

I walk to the patio, see Mim and Winnie in the kitchen.

"Just the girl we want to see," Mim says.

I walk in, sit down at the bright purple table that Mim painted—it's got a huge sunflower design on it. It's impossible to sit at this table and be sad. Mim hands me a strawberry muffin just warm from the oven.

Winnie sips coffee, making those noises adults make when the caffeine starts to kick in. "Anna, did I ever tell you about my grandson Brad?"

"No."

"Well, he's interested in what happened at the library. He's the one who made a phone call and got the police sketch artist to work with us."

"Is he a policeman?"

"He's in a different kind of law enforcement. He's an agent for Homeland Security."

That's going high up!

Mim sits down with her coffee. All three of us are leaning in close at this purple sunflower table.

"Do you know all that Homeland Security does, honey?"

"They look for terrorists."

"That's some of it."

"And they guard the borders . . . and life as we know it . . ." I think that's right.

"You'd be amazed at what they do." Winnie sips her coffee. "I called Brad to tell him our situation, and here's the first question he asked me: Who was in control?"

"What do you mean?"

"Was the girl being controlled by someone, or did it seem she could go where she wanted?"

"The lady had her by the arm. She even went into the bathroom with her."

"So," Winnie says, "the answer is, someone else seemed to be in control of this girl." She takes a big breath. "Brad says that can be a sign of kidnapping, or human trafficking—which is a form of modern-day slavery."

I look at the happy sunflower on this table.

It's not like I live in a cave. I know there are awful things that happen in this world.

But how can something so awful happen here?

"This is tough stuff," Winnie adds. "But if Brad's right . . ."

She lets that hang there.

"What do we do next?" I ask.

"We wait, honey."

"We pray," Mim adds.

I can pray, but I'm not good at waiting.

I write this in my horse journal:

Dear God,

I need you to speed this up because we're pretty sure there are bad guys involved and they need to be stopped!

The other thing is, you've got to help the girl not give up. You've got to do it.

Thank you for horses, grandmothers, librarians, strawberry muffins, and Homeland Security.

Anna M

Fourteen

I'm waiting . . .

First I get a headache.

Then a stomachache.

Then I chew my thumbnails down even more.

I'm doing all this at the long table at Flower People. Burke is hanging around this table, too, not because I'm here. Taylor is sitting next to me.

Right now, he's inspecting mum plants that look fine to me.

Taylor hasn't really looked at him. Me, I just look people in the eye.

Burke takes the mum plants, says, "These are for the library," and heads outside. Taylor watches him through the window. I give her a look, and she says, "Okay, well."

Whatever that means.

Lorenzo says the best part about being twelve is you're close to being a teenager, but you don't have to commit to the whole exhausting experience.

Mom is supposed to call me back this morning, and I don't know how that is going to go.

I keep trying to write something to Dad, but all I can think of to say is:

Please change back. I need a seriously good father right now!

Every kind of flower imaginable is on this table. I'm not great at arranging flowers, but Mim wants to change that. She takes a rose, cuts the stem. "Basically, nature tells us what to do." She puts the rose in a vase and adds some greens. "Flowers don't grow without green, so we need to add that to be natural." Mim clips another rose and places it in the vase. "You don't want them too tall. See? You pick the best flower you've got and make it your focal point."

I take an orange one, Taylor goes for pink. Burke walks by, shakes his head at me. I put the orange flower down, pick up a puffy blue one. Burke nods and walks off.

"Now we build around it." Mim clips flowers quickly and puts them in the vase. "See how easy it is?"

I clip flowers and put them in the vase and it doesn't look anything like Mim's.

Taylor puts three big flowers in a vase surrounded by greens. "Get along, you guys. Make me proud."

Burke laughs from the other room. Taylor smiles slightly. Her design looks much better than mine.

We change and arrange, I stick myself with rose thorns and cut a snapdragon too short. Mim fixes it. "That's pretty good. Stick this here to make it better. See?"

She wraps ribbon around the vase. "That's the ticket."

That's when Mom calls.

"I've been thinking," she says, which can be good or bad, depending.

"Mom, I'm sorry if it seems like I'm not listening to you."

"Anna . . . listen to me." Mom says that she and Mim have been talking, and Mim has explained what's going on with the girl I saw.

"I have to stay, Mom. It's hugely important. I need something that's not about me, you know? I need to help somebody else! I'm not trying to be a pain."

I wait.

Mom sighs. "Honey, I hear you. I understand how important this is. For now, you can stay."

"Mom, thank you!"

"For *now*. But, hear me—if your helping this girl gets out of control, you'll need to come home. You are dealing with a lot of stressful things all at once, whether you know it or not."

Oh, I know it!

My chest feels tight.

"You can't carry all of this on your shoulders, Anna."

"I won't, Mom. Now there's Homeland Security."

"What!"

✿ ✿ ✿

I can't rest at all!

At dinner we light a candle for the girl and pray that God will keep her safe. I want to pray that twelve guys from Homeland Security will drive their tanks to wherever she's at and rescue her. Then she could get adopted by good parents in Philadelphia and we could be friends.

Every day, I promise, I'll think about her.

I'm not going to let this go.

I look at every van I see, whether it's new or scratched. I look in the back window to see if she's there.

I call Daphne a few times to see if anyone has seen her. No one has.

Just me and Winnie.

Everything feels hard.

Everything feels stuck.

Now my brain opens and I remember another thing—not made up—I remember!

The girl had a scar above her eyebrow. I try to draw it.

It was like a squiggle. I remember it now and something else, too.

She had earrings on. They were shaped like little pink flowers. I draw that.

I wish my dad were here, the way he used to be.

I could call him.

Maybe it's a bad time, maybe something made him angry.

Even more reason—he needs to hear an adorable, talented voice.

I speed-dial my father.

Six rings.

I don't want to leave a message. But then, Dad's voice breaks in. "Anna?"

"Dad . . ."

"I am so glad to hear your voice," he says. He doesn't sound angry.

I bite my lip. "It's good to hear yours, too, Dad."

"Wow, kiddo, I'm so sorry I haven't called you."

"It's okay."

"It's not okay. I owe you a big apology. I'm sorry for all the anger, Anna, for all the outbursts . . . I'm sorrier than I know how to say."

"That means a lot, Dad."

"I've been working through a lot of stuff."

I nod—I have, too.

"Tell me . . . how are you doing?"

And we talk about that. How I have one foot here and the other foot there.

We talk about the festival, and then in one long blurt I tell him about the girl in the van, the sheriff, and Homeland Security.

"You've got the big guns on your side! You've got a lot going on."

He sounds like the dad he used to be. . . .

I want to ask, What happened?

Okay, I'm only twelve, but I'm not stupid.

"I wish you were here, Dad."

"I wish I could get away, honey. Work is crazy right now."

I tell him about the yellow scrunchie bracelets.

"Wear that like a flag," he says.

I hold up my hand with the scrunchie. "I will."

"I'm so proud of you, Anna. Prouder than I know how to say."

He used to tell me that all the time.

I'd better not mess up.

✿ ✿ ✿

I'm at the library retracing her steps—how she came in through the front door not on her own, how she was yanked into the bathroom by the lady with the white sunglasses and then pulled out, how she was so brave she tried to escape.

She's got courage, I know it!

I'm in the petunia suit, happy on the outside, wilting on the inside. A lady comes into the library with her baby who won't stop crying. This mother looks so tired. I go up to her and just give her a hug, and she starts crying— they don't prepare you for this in petunia training.

"Can I help, ma'am?"

"I've just had a miserable week." She tries to smile, but her heart isn't in it.

And I do something you're not supposed to do in the

library, but I'm one tough flower and I've learned a thing or two. Actually, I learned this as a radish, about smiling when your heart aches.

That song I sang is perfect for right now. I look at the lady and don't think about my voice cracking or my nerves or any of that.

I just let it come from my heart.

The lady is smiling at me and nodding and her baby is quiet as I sing this song called "Smile."

Ben walks over as I finish, and everyone applauds.

I take a bow. The lady with the baby shakes my hand.

Ben says, "You said you didn't sing."

"Well, only sometimes."

I go back to telling the people about the festival and passing out flyers.

I want to say, *Have you seen a girl with baby animal eyes?* There should be a flyer for that.

It's hot in this suit.

Several kids circle me and do the slide. I try, but . . .

"I can't right now, you guys. I'm sorry. I feel—"

That's all I remember.

I faint dead away.

I wake up on the floor—a crowd of people is looking at me.

"I told you she'd be all right."

I'm not sure who said that.

"What happened?" I ask.

"Low blood sugar," someone guesses.

"The color's coming back to her cheeks."

A pile of festival flyers is on the floor next to me.

"It's going to be fine, darling," Winnie assures me.

"Get her some water."

Ben holds out a bottle of water. I drink.

"Drink some more," he says.

A woman puts her hand on my head. "No fever. You want to go lie down?"

"I am lying down."

Ben laughs. I try smiling. I'm good at this.

Eventually, I get out of the petunia suit and move to the back table. It's quiet here. I'm looking through a book about horses, feeling more relaxed.

A girl with short brown hair is sitting at this table. She's half staring at me, which is irritating.

"Were you a flower?" she asks.

"A petunia." I study a picture of an Appaloosa horse that looks like Zoe. I don't want to talk right now.

"I need to talk to you," she says.

She has a round face with blue eyes and freckles. She leans forward. "You saw that girl who came in here last week with that lady—the one with the flower tattoo?"

I shut the book. "Yes!"

She whispers, "They went in the bathroom together, right?"

"Right."

"And I thought, that's kind of strange."

"Right."

"And the girl was scared."

"You remember her?"

The girl nods. "It just felt weird. The lady she was with smelled like smoke."

I don't remember that exactly.

This girl gets something out of her book bag. A matchbook. She holds it. "I need to tell you something."

My heart is pounding. "Tell me."

"My name's Siri."

"I'm Anna."

"Don't get mad," Siri begs.

"I won't!" I say that louder than you're supposed to in a library. People look at me. Winnie raises an eyebrow. Siri looks scared. "I won't get mad," I whisper.

"I went into the bathroom right after the girl and that lady left, and I found this on the floor." She hands me the matchbook.

It has a silver star that looks just like the star on the lady's pink shirt!

In the middle of the star there's this:

STAR NAILS

And the next part of the address I can't believe!

514 ROSE ST.

ROSEMONT, VA

"WE MAKE YOU A STAR!"

Siri waves her hands. "When I found it, I had to go to my cousin's wedding in Chicago and we were late leaving for the airport. So I couldn't talk to anybody. We just got back and I came right here. I kept trying to tell myself I didn't see anything wrong and I'm not sure I did, but . . ."

"I know," I tell her. "I know exactly what you're saying."

Siri studies the matchbook. "I don't know if the lady who smelled like smoke dropped it or somebody else. Do you think it might be something?"

"It's something, Siri. Believe me."

Fifteen

Winnie puts the matchbook in a clean plastic bag because it could have fingerprints—it's got everyone's fingerprints on it now, but it's good to be careful. Then she sends it by Federal Express to Brad, who says that Siri needs to sit down with Daphne, the police sketch artist.

"I just think I should be there, Bean, but nobody else does. What do you think?" I throw the disgusting ball. He catches it and brings it back. "There's hard stuff in the world, Bean." I throw the ball, Bean jumps up and catches it. "Nice one, boy." I'm about to throw the ball again when another tennis ball rolls past me on the ground. Bean jumps on it, wags his tail, and brings the tennis ball back to Taylor.

What's she doing here?

"I got bored," Taylor says.

I smile and throw my ball and Taylor throws her ball.

Bean is in dog heaven chasing balls and bringing them back again and again.

Taylor shakes her head. "This dog has OCD." She throws her ball. Bean races off to get it. "I heard about the matchbook, Anna." Bean brings the ball back. Taylor throws it.

"Mim says the nail salon opened a year ago," I mention. "That's all she knows. She doesn't get manicures."

I look up to the roof. That's where I need to be. "Come on," I tell Taylor. We climb the ladder to the roof deck.

"Okay, this is amazing," Taylor says.

I throw her a big pillow. "Secret thinking space."

Taylor looks at me, thinking. "How are you doing?"

"I'm not so good at waiting."

"Lost kids have been found based on the tiniest bit of information, Anna."

"I know."

I watch a leaf blow by, dancing on the wind. "Why did you pick missing kids for your report?"

"It's complicated." She sighs. "When my mom died, I kind of lost my dad, too, because he didn't know how to be with me. I just felt like I was missing—a missing girl—and I did the report on missing kids. It was one of the things that helped me. I learned that we have to pay attention to things around us—things that don't feel right.

"You know what you get working with horses? You get this new ability to watch and listen, because a horse is always giving you clues as to how it's feeling. And, it's funny, working with Zoe—who was scared a lot in the beginning, and I was scared, too—I came to see that my dad was scared. I just thought he was cold and self-ish, but he was scared. He didn't know what to do." She looks at me.

I never once thought of my dad as being scared.

Taylor shakes her head. "Here's one of my worst Dad memories. I had to dance with him at his wedding with everyone looking on. I wanted to just burst into tears."

I close my eyes. "I know." I had a bad dance with my dad, an almost dance, actually, at an awful father/daughter fundraiser. Awful because Dad doesn't dance and didn't want to. Awful because so many kids had to dredge up a father substitute for the party. Awful because he and Mom had a big fight before we left.

I always wanted a do-over dance with Dad.

"Did you ever want a different father, Taylor?"

She leans back on her arms and stares straight ahead. "Lots of times."

"Is it bad to want that?"

"It's honest."

"Did you ever have one picked out?"

"Not exactly. Do you?"

I mention Carla Strawlings's dad, who is a widower and a vet and the kindest man I know.

"Vets are excellent role models. My grandma is a vet—retired now. Totally awesome. After Mom died, my dad kept asking me, 'What's wrong with you?' like I was supposed to not be sad. But when I came here, my grandma kept telling me what was right with me and how to build on that."

I blurt out, "I'm scared my parents are going to get divorced."

"Whatever happens, you'll be okay."

"How do you know that?"

She puts her hands behind her head and looks at the clouds moving across the big sky. "Because you're fierce."

I am?

"You can handle anything that comes."

I put my hands behind my head, too, and smile.

Then from the garden I hear, "Are you up there?"

It's Mim, motioning me down.

Taylor and I crawl back to earth on the ladder.

Something's wrong. Mim looks pale. "What happened?" I ask.

"Not much. Brad called the sheriff, who said that Star Nails is run by a man who gives to local charities. . . . He's an upstanding member of the community. . . ."

"What about the girl?"

Mim shakes her head. "The sheriff said his office would continue to look into it."

"We're not trusting the sheriff to do that, right?"

"I don't trust him to do much on this," Mim agrees, "if anything."

Taylor looks at her hands. "My nails are a mess."

I look at her hands. They just look regular to me.

Taylor smiles. "I need a manicure. I hear there's a nail salon on Rose Street run by an upstanding member of the community."

Sixteen

I've never had a manicure, but I decide not to confess.

"Is this a good idea?" I ask from the backseat.

"It's an idea." Mim drives down Rose Street.

Past Crudup's Country Market with the smiling face of Coleman Crudup on a big sign.

Past Crudup's Corner with another big sign: a smiling Coleman Crudup looking at a cow who looks pretty happy, too.

Past the big sign that mentions there are three other Crudup markets in the five-mile area.

Mim drives past Mabel's Place and parks across the street in front of Star Nails.

My heart is racing.

I half expect to see a van with a ripped American flag sticker parked in front, just to make things really clear. I look at the Star Nails building—small and white, with steps leading to a porch. The front door has a silver star on it. I look at the upstairs windows. The pink curtains are closed.

Taylor adjusts her sunglasses. "We are undercover. My name is Bianca."

Oh please.

"You, Anna, are Tess."

"I don't want to—"

"And, Mim, you're—"

"Tired."

We get out of the car.

"Remember everything," Taylor whispers.

"And if at any point one of us doesn't feel safe, we all leave," Mim mentions. "Agreed?"

Agreed.

"Be exceptionally normal," Taylor adds. "And, if possible, boring, so we can blend in."

Mim smiles. "I'm not sure this group is capable of boring."

We walk up the steps, through the pink door with the silver star on it, and into a large room where Asian women are sitting at tables doing nails.

A smiling man walks up. "Family plan?" he asks, laughing.

Taylor elbows me and we start laughing.

"Three manicures," Mim tells him.

"Pick color."

Mim, who doesn't go wild, picks clear, I pick Whisper Pink, and Taylor, after what seems like ages, goes for a glittering red called Crimson Sparkle.

"Will this color glow in the dark?" Taylor asks the man, who doesn't laugh.

I'm looking at every face in this place. I don't see the girl. I'm the only official girl here. Taylor is massively mature.

"Sit, please," the man says to me. He smiles big. He has a gold tooth. "You sad girl today?"

"No, I'm just . . ."

"She's an actor," Taylor explains. "You know. Moody."

Thanks.

He doesn't know moody.

"Everybody happy here," he shouts, and the women who are doing manicures look up and smile. "We make you star," he tells me. "Okay?"

"Sure," I say. I'm looking around for the lady I saw in the van. She isn't here either.

Maybe this whole thing is a joke. Maybe nothing I thought I saw was right.

Mim has one hand soaking in a little bowl.

"What's your name?" she asks the young woman who is cutting her nails.

I can't hear what that woman says.

We're supposed to leave if anyone doesn't feel safe, right?

Except we don't have a signal for that.

Taylor shakes her head at me.

And that means what?

A nail lady in a pink Star Nails shirt examines my hands. She rubs them.

"Soft," she says.

"Thank you."

My nails are supershort and jagged.

"Bite?" she asks.

"I'm sorry?"

She touches my nails. "You bite?"

"Oh, yes, sometimes. It's a bad habit."

"No bite," she says. "Pretty."

She rubs stuff on my nails. I can hear Taylor say, "So where are you from?"

"Vietnam," her nail person answers.

I don't know what to say to my lady.

Seen any girls with baby animal eyes lately?

"Wow," Taylor is saying, "I've always wanted to visit

your country. How long have you been here?"

The woman looks nervously at the man, who comes over. "Girls come to be Americans." He points to an American flag above the cash register. "Very proud."

I gulp. My brain goes to the PROUD TO BE AN AMERICAN sticker on the van.

I don't look at Taylor or Mim or anyone.

"Relax hand," my nail lady says.

"I'm sorry."

"I love Vietnamese food." That's Taylor. "Totally love it."

"You like?" her lady asks.

"The sandwiches, the spring rolls. To die for."

"No die." The man laughs. "Happy!"

The women look up smiling and look back down. The man claps his hands. "Happy!"

I try to memorize every corner of this salon, every face.

"Relax hand," my nail lady says.

"Sorry."

"I drive here every week from Colton," a woman tells Mim. "Best manicure around."

The man smiles at her. "Good customer!"

Sure is happy here, although it doesn't seem real.

"I'm here from San Francisco," Taylor lies. "Have you been there?"

Her nail lady shrugs and looks down.

My nails are looking good—smooth and even. The lady gives me a hand massage and I feel my muscles relax a little.

"Tight," she says, rubbing my thumbs.

"I guess."

More customers come in. Every seat is taken.

The lady paints my nails with Whisper Pink. I love it. She's so careful, like an artist painting. She puts on another coat.

"You star now," she says.

"Thank you."

"Happy!" The man claps.

I put my hands under the dryer. Another lady comes over and gives me a magazine.

"Thank you."

"Nice," she says.

I look at her. She has the biggest eyes. Really huge eyes.

"Nice," she says again.

I look down at the magazine. It's open to a page with

pictures of shoes that have such high heels, they look like they'd kill a person.

"Thank you," I tell her.

There's nothing happening here that I can see.

Nothing that points to this girl.

The nail lady with the big eyes is watching me.

I just want to leave, okay?

We don't exactly have a signal for that!

Taylor and Mim aren't paying attention to me. Mim is talking to the woman next to her like she has all the time in the world. Taylor is lying away: "Yes, I have a career on the stage, but I try to be balanced. I can't say yes to everything."

"Happy!"

I don't think so!

Seventeen

"Shhhh." Taylor holds up her hand as we walk across the street from Star Nails. "Appear normal."

"You're talking about a life on the stage and living in San Francisco!"

Mim points to Mabel's Cafe.

"And what about that happy guy?" I whisper. "And the way all the nail ladies looked up and smiled when he said it and looked back down?"

"Shhh."

"I'm way past that!"

My phone rings. It's Mom.

Big Bad Timing.

Appear normal.

I don't want to go home.

"Hi, Mom," I chirp.

Taylor turns around and mouths, *Be careful*.

"What am I doing? Oh, gee . . . well . . ."

Looking for criminals.

You know, the normal stuff kids do when they visit their grandmother.

"We got manicures, Mom."

"Really? I don't picture your grandmother being the manicure type."

Mim walks into Mabel's Place.

"We're going to eat, Mom."

Do I sound as stressed as I feel?

"Good. Are you relaxing?" Mom asks.

"Wow, you know, it's just amazing what's happening to my muscles here, Mom." I rub my sore neck.

"I'm glad, Anna. You seemed pretty tense when you left."

You should see me now!

"Well, there's not much to report here, honey. I just wanted to hear your voice."

"How are you, Mom? Really."

"Really? . . . Oh, my. Well, I'm glad to not be fighting with your dad all the time. I miss you and the house." She sighs. "And I am really eating too much ice cream."

I laugh. "Go for it, Mom."

"Don't worry. I am."

I tell her, "I'm okay. I want you to know that."

Mom says, "Well, if things gets boring, you can always come home."

"Boring," I assure her, "hasn't happened yet."

Mabel's smells like caramel rolls—that's their specialty. They are huge and we each get one.

Taylor is examining her nails. "This is the best manicure I've ever had."

✿　✿　✿

We sit at a table out back, eating our gooey rolls. It's hard to talk about something bad when you're eating something so good.

I'm trying to remember what I saw. On my napkin I write:

Happy!
NOT

The deputy who did zilch for us is at a table drinking coffee. Now he's picking his teeth.

I write:

```
    74
    16
 + 12
 ─────
   102
```

102 is the combined years Mim, Taylor, and I have been on the earth. We've seen a lot in that time.

One of the things I've seen is this: *when something feels wrong, pay attention, and speak up.*

"Everything in that place," I begin, "felt strange."

"I think we should go back," Taylor suggests, "and get pedicures."

I don't want people touching my feet, and I sure don't want to go back there!

Mim sips her coffee. "What's the purpose of that?"

Taylor holds up a piece of gooey roll—the caramel drips down. "To observe."

"We just did that," I say.

"But now we know what to look for." Taylor pulls her roll apart.

"What would we see that we didn't see?"

The deputy now is scratching his neck, not looking for anybody.

On the napkin, I draw a picture of a van with a girl's head looking out the window. Taylor grabs the napkin and the pen. "She had big eyes, right?"

"Yes."

"Bambi eyes." She draws those.

I take the napkin back and write above the picture.

HAVE YOU SEEN HER?

I'm not letting this go.

❀ ❀ ❀

Coleman Crudup isn't letting things go either.

He's creeping around town trying to become the sponsor for the festival.

"*Sorry,*" Mim tells him.

The parade is six days away. I'm going to march as a petunia, but also be a deputy petal person and manage twelve little kids dressed as flowers.

He wants to "donate" money so that his daughter's band (that's the middle school jazz band) can have the number one slot in the parade. He'll buy all the flowers for his stores from Mim if she'll just "bend a little."

"*No, sir,*" says Mim.

There's an ugly side to a flower festival.

At the library, I hear Caitlin apologize to Ben. "Daddy always wants me to be first. I told him, I don't want that!"

Points for Caitlin.

Coleman Crudup is meeting with the mayor, meeting with the tourism council, running ads in the newspapers of nearby towns all to promote "our little festival."

"He's hitting everywhere at once," Burke explains. "He's giving donations to every organization in town who'll take it."

"How many take the money?" Taylor asks.

"More than we'd like."

Flower madness hits Rosemont. Big trucks delivering flowers for the festival are everywhere in town. In the old factory building, an air-conditioning truck pushes cold air into the huge space to keep the thousands of flowers fresh. People wear crazy flower hats; Merv, who oversees the float building in the hangar, wears a cowboy hat with plastic flowers that blink.

This town is getting ready.

I am, too.

I'm back in the petunia suit, by the front door of the library, when Coleman Crudup marches in. He looks at me and laughs. I curtsey. I'm supposed to be adorable to everyone.

"You're Mim's granddaughter, aren't you?" he asks.

"Yes, sir." I do a twirl. "But today I am a petunia."

"What's your name?"

"Anna."

He's liking this. "Annie, you've got personality."

"It's Anna—"

"How much are you getting paid for this?"

"I'm doing it for free, to help the library."

Hands on his hips. "I'll pay you serious bucks to do this at my market."

Ben walks by wearing a shirt that reads RENT A GENIUS.

I like the serious bucks part, but not the person who would be giving me the money.

"I can get you a better costume—we'll have it made today. You can be a strawberry." He smiles. "What do you say?"

I look over at Ben, who isn't smiling. I don't want to talk to Coleman Crudup anymore, but he takes out his wallet, rips out a fifty-dollar bill, and hands it to me. "Earnest money, Annie. I'd like you to work for me."

"I can't . . ."

"Of course you can." He walks into the library. I look at the fifty-dollar bill. President Grant is on the front, not smiling, like Ben.

"This note is legal tender for all debts, public and private."

I can do a lot with fifty dollars.

I hear Coleman Crudup tell another man, "We're going to get this show on the road in a big way."

He sweeps through the door, and turns back to me. "There's more where that came from." He hands me his business card.

"Sir, I can't take—"

"It's yours, Annie. Give your grandmother my regards."

I don't think I'll be doing that.

And off he goes.

I don't know what to do with this money, and being a petunia I don't have a pocket. Ben walks over.

"He gave me fifty dollars. I told him not to." I point to Ben's shirt, RENT A GENIUS. "How much do you charge?"

"The first consultation is free."

We walk out of the library past the hedges shaped like animals.

"How well do you know this town, Ben?"

"I was born here." He turns down Wisteria Lane.

"How well do you know Crudup?"

"Not too many people stand up to him and win."

I think about Mim standing tough. I hope she doesn't get knocked down.

"I have a statement to make, Anna. We still need a singer for the band. Practice is in seventeen minutes."

"But . . ."

"I wrote a song you can sing. Come on."

❖   ❖   ❖

There are twelve kids in the band, plus the bandleader, Mr. Cole.

"We call him Mr. Cool," Ben says. This fits him.

Caitlin is blowing spit out of her trumpet and glaring at me. *Nice to see you, too.*

Mr. Cool is looking at Ben's music. "Okay, guys, we've got a blues number here by one of our own."

The band nods.

Mr. Cool smiles at me. "And it looks like we've got a singer."

The band nods again and says, "Yeah . . ."

I cough. "Actually, I'm just visiting."

Ben shoves the music into my hands. The song is called "Tell Me," words and music by Ben Adler.

Wow.

I've never known a songwriter before, except for me, but I write mine on the spot, not on paper.

Ben hands Caitlin the music. "It's got a good trumpet part. You get a solo." She looks at the music.

"Listen up." Mr. Cool plays the melody on the piano. He looks at Ben. "Now that's good, son." To everyone, he says, "Here's how it goes," and sings the first few lines.

Tell me how you're doing,
I really want to know.
Are you feeling good
Or are you feeling low?

Mr. Cool laughs. "Can we get that groove?"

The band scrunches up their faces and looks at the new music. I'm getting seriously nervous about singing. My throat is getting dry. I'm coughing.

Mr. Cool snaps his fingers, "Together now, one, two, three, four . . ."

They play, but not together.

It sounds awful. Ben looks down.

"Okay, first time is guaranteed bad. We're over that." Mr. Cool snaps his fingers again. It still sounds pretty bad, except for Caitlin's trumpet. She's good. He looks at me. "Anna, I'll play, you sing."

Uh . . .

I don't normally sing this way, but Mr. Cool doesn't give me a choice. He plays an intro, points to me. I give it my best.

Tell me how you're doing,
I really want to know.
Are you feeling good
Or are you feeling low?

Mr. Cool twirls his finger in the air. I don't know what that means, so I stop.

We work on this song again and again until it's sounding decent.

Tell me if it's bad for you.
Tell me what you need.
I'm your friend.
You can count on me.

"Anna," Mr. Cool says, "sing behind the beat on the *you can count on me*. You can uh uh count on me. Try it."

You can uh uh count on me.

Everybody laughs.

The *uh uh* was supposed to be silent.

I try it again, again.

"Anna," Mr. Cool says, "keep your head up."

I don't really want to look at people.

"And remember," he says, "your vocal cords are strong. They like it when you sing out."

I gulp, put my hand over my neck.

Mr. Cool snaps his fingers: *"One . . . two . . . three . . . take it."*

I get it this time. It's sounding halfway good, almost like I'm a real singer.

"Do it again," Mr. Cool says, and this time Caitlin plays her solo.

That sounds good!

I add:

Oh yeah . . .
You can count on me!

Caitlin and I finish exactly on time.

I smile at her. She doesn't smile back exactly, but she doesn't seem like she hates me either.

I'll take that.

Mr. Cool says the band should play this at the parade.

The thing is . . . I raise my hand.

"I won't be able to sing with you. I'm a deputy petal person and I've got to march with twelve little kids."

Ben is disappointed.

Mr. Cool says they'll just do the instrumental.

It's a good song, Ben.

I wish I could sing with you.

And, Caitlin, you're the best player in the band.

You probably already know that.

Eighteen

"It's pedicure time," Taylor says, wiggling her toes.

"I've been meaning to get a pedicure for about twenty years," Mim adds.

I've never even thought about having a pedicure.

I gobble up the last of my caramel roll and we walk out of Mabel's.

Mim, Taylor, and I head across the street to Star Nails.

Up the stairs.

Through the door with the silver star.

We're baaaaack . . .

"Happy!"

"Beyond happy," Taylor assures him.

The man claps his hands. "Good customers, special price! Pick color."

I want to match. I find the Whisper Pink. Taylor searches through the polish. "I am such a contradiction, my toes should be blue, I think."

Mim picks rose.

We sit in the chairs, put our feet on risers. The women who work here take such care to do a good job. I like them.

I'm feeling so many things.

My nail lady washes my feet, which is weird. She smoothes the bottom of my foot with a file and I break out laughing.

She smiles. "Tickle?" She uses the file again.

I laugh and twist in the chair. Is this part of the pedicure? Taylor and Mim aren't laughing. The lady does it to me again. I laugh hard. Everyone smiles.

"Happy!" The man comes over to me. "You more happy now." He smiles at me and gives me a rose from a vase. "For most happy girl."

"Thank you." He's kind of nice, actually.

The nail lady starts up with my other foot and I fall apart.

"So much for blending in," Taylor mutters.

I guess spies aren't supposed to be ticklish.

This is a pretty place, all pink and white with stars and flowers; this is a clean place.

The Happy! man goes outside to smoke.

So, what am I looking for?

What's going on here?

The lady with the big eyes who gave me the magazine when I had my manicure stands in the corner watching.

My nail lady puts paper sandals on my feet. She smoothes and shapes my toenails and paints them Whisper Pink.

Honestly, these don't look like my feet at all.

I get out of the chair, head to the foot dryer. Walking in these sandals makes me waddle like a duck. If we have to run for our lives, I'm in trouble.

I stick my feet under the dryer. I wait, watch.

I want to go up to every nail lady, show them the napkin drawing, and shout:

HAVE YOU SEEN HER?

Mim and Taylor waddle over now, and we sit in a line drying our toes. I'm dying to ask them if they saw anything new.

The nail lady with the big eyes walks over to me quickly and hands me a magazine like last time. "Nice," she says. She pats the magazine.

"Thank you."

She turns the page for me, and there is a little blue envelope. She touches the envelope quickly and looks at me. Her eyes are big and scared.

It's almost like—

Now Taylor, who is sitting next to me, sees the envelope. She sucks in air.

My phone buzzes.

I jump.

The magazine drops.

The envelope hits the floor.

I CAN'T BELIEVE THIS!

Instantly, I put my foot over the envelope, which isn't easy. I'm now slipping out of the chair.

Taylor grabs hold of me.

People are looking. "She's young," Taylor says. "Her first pedicure."

I smile and wave at people, trying to seem normal twisted up like a pretzel.

I can't take my foot off the envelope! I try to move it toward me slowly.

Inch by inch.

Almost.

And now my foot is cramping.

"Everyone," Taylor whispers, "is watching us."

"Do something weird," I whisper back.

Taylor instantly laughs way too loud. Everyone looks at her, and I scoop up the envelope.

There's no place to put it fast except down my shirt!

So I do.

Wow.

I clamp my hand over my chest to keep it there.

I don't dare look at the nail lady with the big eyes.

I'm sure everyone saw everything I just did.

Mim says a little loudly, "Now what would you girls like for dinner tonight?"

"Hmmm," Taylor says. "Now let me think about that."

I pat my chest in time to the music that's playing, nod my head.

"Pizza!" Taylor shouts.

"Oh, yes." I'm still patting myself to the music.

I look at Mim, make my best *we so need to get out of here* expression.

We stand up, I feel the envelope drop lower in my

shirt. I'm patting my stomach now. Let me tell you, it's not easy to get my real shoes on!

"Bye-bye," Mim says. "Thank you."

"Bye, star ladies!"

✿ ✿ ✿

I'm walking down the street with Mim and Taylor, and I'm whispering about the envelope. Only whispering, and Mim says, "Not here."

I'm pretty sure that everyone is looking at me.

I start humming the "Smile" song written by Charlie Chaplin, who had to get a lot of information across just using his face.

I roll my eyes at Taylor, who doesn't get that I mean

DEEP AND POSSIBLE DANGER

As in . . .

ARE WE BEING FOLLOWED BY BAD GUYS?

I'm sure we are.

Which of us will turn around first to check?

Mim does. "We're fine."

Speak for yourself.

My heart is rolling in my chest, causing the envelope in my shirt to shake.

"I feel a little dizzy," I mention.

Mim takes my arm.

We walk to the car and get in. Mim starts the engine, and we're off.

Taylor shouts, "Tell me everything, Anna, with unerring detail."

"I don't have any detail yet. I haven't read the note!"

I take the wrinkled envelope from my shirt, try to smooth it.

There are letters on the note with accent marks, drawn with black ink.

This isn't English. I hand it to Taylor. "Is this Chinese?"

She looks at it while Mim drives. "I think it's some kind of Asian writing."

"Okay," I say, "now someone better pay attention."

"Hold on." Mim makes a sharp turn and heads down the street fast.

"Are we going to the sheriff's?" I ask.

"Absolutely not."

She speeds around a corner, turns right, left, right, and cuts through to the back end of the library.

I look around. "Why are we at the library?"

Mim slaps the dashboard. "This is where things get done!"

Nineteen

Mim jumps out of the pickup. Taylor and I do, too. We slam our doors at exactly the same time, march up the front steps, and head for the return desk.

Winnie stops what she's doing.

Taylor hands her the note.

"Is this Vietnamese?" Mim whispers.

Winnie puts her finger to her mouth.

Shhhhh . . .

She heads to the back, and we follow her up the stairs, to the right, where she reaches for a book on a high shelf. She opens it, lays the note on it.

"You see these symbols? They're similar. I think you're right, Mim. This is Vietnamese."

She looks at Taylor and me. "What can you tell me?"

I look around and whisper about what happened at Star Nails.

Winnie nods.

I mention the size of the lady's eyes.

"Maybe she's related to the girl," Winnie suggests.

I hadn't thought of that!

She whips out her phone, punches a button. "Agent Brad Dugan, please . . . He's in a meeting? . . . Yes, it's extremely important." She stands tough. "Tell him his grandmother is calling!"

☆ ☆ ☆

Winnie makes copies of the Vietnamese note and sends the original to Brad, who is going to have it translated and probably dusted for fingerprints, or whatever it is they do to fight evil.

"It's official," she tells us. "Brad is opening a full investigation. That boy can find a button at the bottom of the sea."

Taylor yells, "Woo-hoo!" which is the right thing to shout, but not in the library.

"I have something to say." Winnie puts her hands on her hips and glares at me, Mim, and Taylor. "I can't believe you went to Star Nails without me!"

"We could have used a librarian," Mim mentions.

Winnie snaps, "Remember that next time."

"We won't be going back there," Mim says.

I think about what Lorenzo told me:

She's lucky it was you who saw her, Anna. You won't let it go.

I should have done more.

But what?

Mim walks over. "You need a break, Anna."

"I can't—"

"You need a break," Mim says.

Taylor says, "Listen to your grandmother."

I shake my head.

The van was scratched.

The people were Asian.

The lady was wearing a pink shirt with a silver star.

The girl was wearing . . .

What?

What was she wearing?

My brain closes up.

Mim takes my hand. "You need a break, Anna. That's an order."

✿　✿　✿

"Ohhh . . ."

That's all I can say.

I feel my hair go electric frizz from the humidity. There are trees, a little path, so many flowers, and the butterflies—you can't believe how many.

"It's year-round now," Mim says. An orange butterfly flits in her face. She smiles at it. We're in the Rosemont Butterfly House, and every color of butterfly is here— they drink from hanging feeders, get juice from cut-up oranges. A pink one flutters past. I hold out my hand, and it lands on my thumb.

"Hi," I whisper. "I'm totally honored you chose me." The butterfly stays for a minute, then flies off.

A monarch butterfly flits right in Taylor's face. "I'm going to name you Fluffy," Taylor says to it. "Can you handle that?"

Guess not. The butterfly takes off.

Taylor calls after it. "How about Seymour?"

Taylor is sitting on a rock by a waterfall looking like a little kid. It's impossible to be stressed in a butterfly house.

I grin at Mim. "Thank you."

She nods, *you're welcome.*

And if I had to write a paper for English, which I

don't because it's summer, I would write about how good things sometimes light on you for just a minute, but their touch stays with you.

I feel peace—I need that.

I feel warmth—I need that.

"You're relaxed?" Mim asks.

I nod.

"Are you ready for the next part?"

❀   ❀   ❀

"Don't lean over when you sit her. Taller, girl. That's it. Chin up."

Dr. Gudrey, Taylor's grandmother, tells me this. She and Mim are standing by the riding ring watching, but I get the better deal.

I'm riding Zoe! This might be my greatest moment ever, with the exception of when I got a standing ovation as a radish. Being on this horse makes me feel like I'm on top of everything big that could hurt me.

"Now, she wants to understand you," Dr. Gudrey says as calm as anything. "What do you want to do?"

"I want to go faster."

"That would be a trot. In a minute you'll give her a gentle press with your foot, and as she moves into it, find the rhythm and rise and fall with her."

"Okay, girl, let's go." I press slightly with my foot, and she picks up the pace. I'm not sure how to go up and down, and I think she might be going too fast. "Whoa," I say. And instantly Zoe stops. "No, not that kind of whoa." I'm laughing now.

I press my foot, feel Zoe click into the trot. I feel the way to go up and down with her. It's like I'm part of this animal.

"You're a natural, Anna!" Dr. Gudrey says.

How cool is this!

I go round and round the ring. I never want to get off this horse.

Mim smiles like she knew I had it in me all the time.

Thank you, Mim. Thank you for knowing what I need!

"Now," Dr. Gudrey says, "I want you to take it to a canter, Anna. Press with your foot and she'll go a little faster and it will be smoother."

Faster is smoother?

I press and she does speed up. Maybe too much? Did we skip cantering and go right to galloping?

"You're looking strong," Dr. Gudrey calls.

"Zoe, I hope you know what you're doing."

Zoe likes the canter. At first I'm bouncing up and

down like crazy, but Dr. Gudrey calls, "Find her rhythm, Anna. Up, down, up . . . that's it. Like sitting in a rocking chair."

I'm bumping, but that's how it is when you're learning something new, bumping along, trying to remember all the things you're supposed to do in your head, and they all swirl in your mind as you try to grab each one and do it and then the next and the next . . .

And then there's that moment when you get it. You're free.

I'm grinning. I love this!

I don't think about anything else. The dust kicks up under Zoe's feet, my hair flies back in the wind, the sun is shining, the sky is pale blue, and I'm doing it, I'm really riding.

Now I see Taylor watching me, and she shouts, "Yeah, Anna. Ride!"

Twenty

I burst through Mim's front door, an official rider who just rode the best horse ever, and that's when I freeze.

"I can't believe it!" I shout.

I'm not kidding. Dad is sitting in the hugging chair!

He leaps up when he sees me and gives me a hug that no chair on earth can give.

Dad laughs deep. "Surprise!"

I look at his face.

He doesn't look angry.

I look in his eyes. They don't seem upset.

He's laughing now, like he used to.

"Dad, I didn't expect—"

"Well, it just seemed like the right place to be."

Mim is standing in the hall and she's smiling at Dad like she's lit by the sun.

"Old girl," he says to her, "it's been too long." And they hug like it's been too long, which it has.

Mim's laughing. "Brian McConnell, what in the world are you doing here?"

"I took some vacation and found myself heading for Rosemont."

Mim looks at him. "You look pale."

Dad says, "So do you."

"Don't be fresh. Have you eaten?"

He laughs. "I'd never eat before coming here, you know that."

"We're going to fatten you up."

Dad puts an arm around me and one around Mim. And something feels like old times. "God, it's good to see you."

Dad laughs deep as we walk into the kitchen.

What's going on around here?

✿ ✿ ✿

We eat until we're almost sick. Apple sausage, cheddar cheese, chewy dark bread, potato salad, and grapes. There are brownies left from yesterday, and I cut a big one for Dad and give him a frosty glass of milk the way he likes it. I tell him about riding Zoe.

"I was so careful. Honest, Dad."

"I know how much you love horses, Anna."

He doesn't look mad, and believe me, I'm watching.

I sit there. I don't want to break the magic.

I don't want to ask, or ruin the moment by saying the wrong, dumb thing like . . .

What's going on?

Why are you here, Dad?

Why are you happy?

Dad and Mim are talking about the festival and he laughs, remembering when she started it twenty years ago.

"You had three gardens set up for people to visit. I remember."

"You helped plant all the petunias that year."

Hey, that's my flower.

"Those were good times, honey," Mim tells him.

Dad leans back. "I'm trying to find those times again." He looks at me. "And I didn't want to miss the excitement here." He looks at his hands. "I don't know how to say it. I'm sorry. I've been awful this year."

I look at Mim, who says, "We love you, you know that."

"I don't deserve it, but I'll take it."

"Hold on now," Mim says. "What's this about not deserving love?"

"Mother, I didn't mean . . ."

"Because if you think you're loved only when you're acting perfect, we're all in trouble."

Dad's still looking at his hands. "I know . . . it hit me hard that I've got to change."

It's so quiet in this room, like we're all holding our breath.

"Dad, tell me again about when you fought for the stoplight."

And he tells the story I've heard a thousand times about the dangerous intersection in his neighborhood where two kids were hit by cars. "People wrote it off, they said it was driver error—it was, but there needed to be a stoplight there, to make things safer. The people who owned houses near the corner didn't want a stoplight, and people fought the cost, but, you know, we just went and talked to people, we let them know what we believed, and after a while we got a little army behind us." Dad's face beams. "A little army that really cares can beat a big one."

I love thinking about that.

"They called me a community activist after that, and I never felt that was the right word. I was just a guy who saw things that were wrong and tried to do something about them. That's how I met your mom."

I know this story, too. Mom was working at Town Hall and Dad kept coming in with all the things he needed to change. He laughed. "After I met your mom, I was looking for any little thing that needed changing, so I had an excuse to see her. I'm told I was becoming a real pain."

And now they're apart.

We sit there quietly, but Bean knows what to do. He drops his stinking tennis ball in Dad's lap. Dad picks it up. "I've missed you, buddy, not the ball." Dad goes out back and throws that ball until Bean is too tired to care.

It's settled. Dad will stay with us this week. He'll sleep on the pull-out couch in the living room.

Dad keeps walking outside to the garden, even though it's late, smelling the flowers. Just smelling them.

"Something about all these flowers," he says.

I show Dad the composite drawings that Daphne did. "I'm proud of you, Anna, for not letting this go."

"I feel like I've let it go. Nothing much happening."

"You know what I've learned? In every fight for something important, there's always a time when it feels like nothing's happening."

I write that down and put it under my pillow and wonder how long it takes Homeland Security to translate a note.

❀　❀　❀

I wake up to my father's loud laugh coming from the garden.

I'm getting in on this joy. I head outside in my dog pajamas. Dad and Mim are having a time, drinking coffee, eating muffins. The birds are flying in and out of their houses. I sit down with them. Dad grabs my hand. He's talking about when he helped an animal shelter get the word out about all the dogs they had for adoption. I remember the open house and the people who came to adopt the dogs. That's how we found Peanut.

I'm thinking I should call Mom and tell her that things are changing for Dad and he's not angry right now, and maybe she shouldn't be spending so much time in New Jersey with all those weird painted eggs that are in every room of Uncle Barry's house.

But Mim says to get dressed.

We've got work to do.

That's when Dad hands me a bag. "I figured you didn't need chocolate."

I open it.

I can't believe it!

Inside it are yellow scrunchies.

"I could only find twelve, Anna, but it's a start."

Twenty-One

Burke gets a scrunchie and puts it on his wrist.

Ben gets one, and several kids from the band want to wear them. Everyone is here working on floats.

Now Caitlin Crudup walks up. She wants a scrunchie, too.

"It's not for your hair, Caitlin. It's to remember."

"I know. Ben told us. I want to remember her."

I'm not sure about this.

"Ben told me what you did, Anna." She holds out her hand like she deserves it.

I hand her one. She puts it on her wrist.

"Thank you," she whispers.

✿ ✿ ✿

I can't get enough of this hangar. I'm walking with Mim and Dad, watching the work get done on the floats. So many volunteers have showed up to help.

"You should have seen this place months ago," Merv tells me. He manages the work on all the floats. "It was a sea of chicken wire. And now!"

A man covers the side of a float with dried flowers, moving like a machine. "That's nice," Mim tells him. "I love the textures."

A girl about my age is gluing small beans in circles to outline butterfly wings on the Harvey Mutt Plumbing, Ltd., float. Their theme is "Life Is Good," and you wouldn't normally think of butterflies, rainbows, and hearts as big plumbing symbols, unless you had a toilet that kept overflowing and you know how good life seemed after the plumber fixed it.

This girl keeps laying bean after bean down, making something so beautiful.

"You're doing a fine job," Mim tells her.

She lights up and grins.

All this attention to detail, it pays off.

Mim looks tired. She sits next to a waving chipmunk on the side of the Harvey Mutt Plumbing, Ltd., float as Coleman Crudup walks past fast like he's the King of the Festival.

He looks back and shouts, "You take care of your health, Mim. Nothing more important than that."

Of course, the fact that he shouted it makes everyone look at Mim and wonder.

Well, let them look!

Coleman Crudup points to the floats being decorated. "That's coming along fine, real fine."

"Where's your float, Coleman?" That's Merv asking.

"Oh, I got it hid away."

"You adhering to the rules, friend?" Merv asks.

"Course I am." He slaps Merv on the shoulder.

Merv slaps his shoulder right back. "Gonna have to inspect it, Coleman."

"I'm busy as all get-out, Merv."

Dad sticks out his hand to Crudup. "Brian McConnell, Mim's son."

Crudup nods at that.

"I'll be stepping in and taking care of a few festival issues for her this week. First order of business, sir, is we need to schedule a walk-through of your float and the materials you're using."

Crudup looks surprised. "Well, I'm planning to keep it under wraps until the big day. I'm sure you understand the value of not letting the world in on what you're doing."

"Oh, I understand it," Dad says, "but that's not what this parade is about. You signed an agreement regarding this walk-through and we aim to make sure you abide by that."

Crudup looks a little nervous. "You're just like your mother."

"Thank you," Dad says.

❀   ❀   ❀

More and more volunteers are pouring into Rosemont. The parade is four days away.

Winnie is on the phone, writing something down. "I'll tell them. Yes, I understand."

She motions Dad, Mim, and me into the library conference room.

"That was Brad. They've checked the note you received at the nail salon, Anna."

"What did it say?"

Winnie sighs. "Brad can't tell us."

"Why not?"

"Because it's part of an investigation and he can't talk about the case. He said we sit tight."

Every muscle in my neck might snap, it's so tight!

"What else did he say?"

"These things are carefully planned," Winnie explains.

"He said that?"

"No." Winnie looks at me.

"But what else did he say?"

"He said nothing else."

"And that's okay with everyone?" I'm shouting now.

"It has to be," Dad says.

"This is highly confidential," Winnie adds.

I know that! "What do you think is happening, Winnie?"

Winnie puts her arm around me. "I believe you've given them a powerful piece of evidence and they are going to track this down."

That tells me nothing. Adults are supposed to know things!

Librarians are supposed to know more things than regular people!

I'm in a room with a librarian and two other adults and *I'm sick of not knowing*!

Twenty-Two

Mim's got a pork roast in the oven and potatoes au gratin. Taylor is setting the table—she begged to come to this dinner.

Dad is making the salad, cutting vegetables with all his force, shaking his special vinaigrette with a touch of Dijon mustard in a jar.

I don't remember seeing him like this for ages.

Mim is looking paler than I'd like to see her. Dad's looking better.

I just can't stand it. I step outside and call my mother.

"Well, hi. What a nice surprise!"

I need to get right to it. "Dad's here."

"Oh?"

"And he's different, Mom. He's laughing and he's really helping and he's not going, you know . . ."

"Overboard?" she says sarcastically.

"Yes, but no kidding. Something's happening. I think he saw the light!"

"Anna, I'm glad you're seeing your father in a new—"

"We're all seeing it. It's like how he used to be."

"I hear that. I'm happy for you. I haven't seen it."

"You need to see it."

"Honey . . ."

The doorbell rings. Taylor shouts, "I just spilled the vinaigrette!"

"On my shoes!" Dad adds.

"I've got to go, Mom. We're having company for dinner."

"Who's coming?"

"Homeland Security."

"*What?*"

❀   ❀   ❀

Mim said I'm supposed to be cool at dinner, meaning I'm not supposed to ask Brad specific questions, because he can't talk about the case. I could never work at Homeland Security—Lorenzo would make me tell all. I pass the bread to Brad and say, "So, a while ago you told Winnie that this might all be a sign of"—I gulp—"human trafficking. Could you tell me more about that?"

Mim glares at me. I'm not talking specifics!

Brad says, "Well, it's a big issue. If you think slavery is history, you need to think again."

We all stop eating.

"Sadly, it's in more places than people realize. One of the things we do is work with local authorities to bring the people who victimize others to justice."

Mim passes the buttermilk rolls, Brad takes two more, and I blurt out everything about the nail salon and the Happy! guy and the nail ladies who smile like robots.

Brad leans forward. "Anna, here's what I can tell you. If more people opened their eyes like you've done, it would wake others up to what's going on." Brad looks at all of us. "Sometimes a thing you see can seem so small. And you think, Who would be interested in that?"

"The sheriff here wasn't," Winnie mutters.

"He is now." Brad takes more pork from the platter. "I can tell you stories of the littlest clue that led to hundreds of people being freed and the people who held them going to jail."

"For how long?" Taylor asks.

"They won't be getting out."

Good.

I think of hundreds of girls with baby animal eyes being set free.

"We're looking for patterns," Brad explains. "We track this everywhere. We know what it looks like." He hands me his business card. "If you see anything else, tell me."

Bean, the ever-hopeful dog, comes in with his ball.

"Not now," Taylor tells him.

But hope knows how to wait. Bean wags his tail and sits there.

"Do you guys work with, like, the FBI?" Taylor asks.

"And the CIA, the Department of Defense, the Department of Justice, the Department of the Treasury, the National Counterterrorism Center, the National Security Staff, U.S. Customs—just to name a few."

Winnie pats his arm. "Brad always got along with different kinds of people."

Brad laughs. "You're looking pretty sharp these days, Grandma. You read any good books lately?"

Winnie mentions ten titles fast.

"I'll look into the one about training terrorists in . . . where was it?"

"Boise. I'll have it for you at the library. You can consider it an interlibrary loan, but I want it back in three weeks. Don't mess with me on this, and no bullet holes in it."

"Yes, ma'am." Brad smiles like the superhero he is, and has thirds.

✿   ✿   ✿

Winnie and Brad leave, and Taylor says, "I swear, Anna, I have never felt so safe in my entire life as I did at dinner with Brad."

Taylor says "Brad" with extra meaning.

"You like him."

She walks off. "I'm glad he's on the job."

"He's too old for you!"

"I know. And the reality of that is beyond bleak."

"What about Burke?"

Taylor makes a noise.

✿   ✿   ✿

When Homeland Security is on the case, there's not much for a kid to do.

I do the dishes with Taylor.

I play cards with Dad.

I look at the composite drawings and look at them again to see if I missed anything.

I know this much.

That girl needs hope.

How do you send hope to a kid when you don't know where she is?

I get paper and write:

KEEP HOPING

THINGS ARE HAPPENING

I'm not as good an artist as Taylor, but I draw a white dove over the HOPING.

Taylor walks over eating the last brownie. She studies my paper, points to the bird. "What's that?"

"You know, a dove of hope."

She eats some more. "It's the dove of peace, not hope."

I'm defending my work. "This is a hope dove."

She raises the last bite of brownie. "There is no designated animal for hope, Anna. Doves are always for peace."

I write:

KEEP UP THE PEACE

THINGS ARE HAPPENING

Sometimes editing makes things worse.

I go back to hope, although I need an official hope animal.

Robins are hopeful . . .

Kittens . . .

Dolphins . . .

Otters . . .

Then Bean trots in with his mangy tennis ball, so hopeful that someone will play with him.

I laugh. "Bean, how would you like to be the official hope dog?"

Bean wags his tail and accepts.

"An old dog with a disgusting ball might not go mainstream, Anna."

I take a picture of Bean with my phone. "It might."

"I have to go. It's been an amazing evening." Taylor sighs, puts her hand over her heart.

I giggle.

"Was that necessary, Anna?"

❀　❀　❀

I'm so tired that I fall asleep on top of my bed with my clothes on.

At two a.m. there's a knock at my bedroom door.

"Anna, wake up." It's Dad. "We've got a problem here." I shake sleep from my head. "We need to get your grandmother to the hospital."

What?

I'm already dressed. I run into the hall. Dad is helping Mim put on a sweater. She's looking pale.

"This is nothing, Brian. Just a little fluttering in my heart."

"Mother, let's let the doctor tell us that, okay?"

Mim's fussing with her purse. "I can't be messing around at a hospital right now. The parade starts in thirty-two hours."

"You know what, Mom?" Dad takes her by the arm and walks her to the car. "This one you don't get to decide."

I climb into the back of Dad's car. My mouth is so dry. He drives to the hospital. I don't know what to say. I feel like I've got something on my chest that's making it hard for me to breathe.

"This is all just a fuss," Mim says.

Nothing can be wrong with her.

Nothing!

Twenty-Three

In the hospital waiting room. Every minute feels an hour long. I feel like marching up and telling the nurse at the desk just how important Mim is, in case they haven't figured it out.

How can someone like Mim who has such a big heart have a heart problem?

It doesn't make sense.

I don't care about the parade or the festival.

I'm mad at Crudup, who probably hurt Mim's heart by being the jerk that he is.

My heart's feeling tight, now it's racing a little. I put my hand over my chest and breathe in and out slow.

The doctor checks Mim's heart. He makes her cough. They do a test; they do some more. More hours pass.

Waiting.

It's seven in the morning when a doctor says, "She

can go home, looks like stress. She needs to rest."

Mim makes a that's-not-possible sound about resting.

"She'll rest," Dad tells the doctor.

Mim isn't happy about that. "Well, somebody better call Burke and let him know, and tell him that he and Merv have full rein to manage the volunteers. I can't be there till a little later."

The doctor and Dad look at her.

"I've had people working all night, and I'm not going to desert them now."

Not leaving it alone runs in the family.

✿　✿　✿

We bring Mim home, and she informs us, "I'm perfectly fine and I don't want all of you looking at me like a dam that's about to bust. I hate being a bother." She heads to her room.

"You're not a bother," I say after her.

Dad yawns. "I'd better get over to the hangar and make sure Crudup doesn't take over the world."

I might just sit here.

I sure don't feel like decorating a float.

Right now, I don't care about this parade or this

festival and Crudup and his cruddy grocery stores. I just want to sit here and make sure Mim's all right.

I walk by her room. The door is open a little. I stand outside watching her.

"What is it?" she snaps.

"I just wondered if you were all right."

"I've been in here for five minutes, Anna."

A lot can happen in five minutes!

It's clear that watching her will drive her crazy.

I wonder if Brad and his squadron of Homeland Security people are awake.

I wonder if there's anything I can do anywhere in this town that will help somebody.

Bean comes up with his ball and drops it.

"Not now, Bean."

He pushes it toward me with his nose and looks so hopeful.

I take the ball outside and throw it, and this old dog leaps for a perfect catch again and again.

"This is boring, Bean."

He wags his tail. He was made to do this.

What was I made to do anyway?

Brad told me to keep watching.

There's nothing to look at here.

But wait a minute!

This idea I just got, it involves making my father very angry.

Dad's in the shower right now.

I write him a note, stick it near the coffeepot. He'll always see it there.

> I'll meet you at the hangar, Dad. I need to do
> something first.
> Love,
> Anna

✿　✿　✿

I'm walking down Rose Street. The stores are waking up. Crudup's Country Market is open for business, with a big picture of Caitlin's dad giving a thumbs-up standing next to a cow statue covered with flowers. Good smells float out of Mabel's Cafe, which has flowering trees on either side of the door. I so want to go in, but this isn't the time to think about caramel rolls, even though they're warm and gooey and right here.

I've got a job to do.

I'm across from the Star Nails salon, which has flowered star wreaths hanging in every window, making it hard to see inside. It's eight seventeen in the morning, too early for them to be open. The pink curtains in the upstairs windows are closed.

I don't know what I'm looking for, but I'm looking.

A ping on my phone. It's Dad.

Where are you?

I answer back: Rose Street. I'm fine.

An irritated ping.

Are you anywhere near the nail salon?

Kind of.

Come home, Anna. Right now.

In a minute.

I swear, I'm never like this!

Maybe Homeland Security can swoop down and get the job done so I can obey my father.

Did you hear me, Anna?

Yes sir. I'm safe. I need to watch.

I stay right where I am, watching. If anything happens, I can run into Mabel's.

And now my phone rings.

"Hi, Dad."

"Anna, I am in the car coming to pick you up, and I promise, I am not happy."

"I know, Dad."

I'm watching the salon. No signs of anything inside or out.

Where are you exactly???????

By Mabel's.

I wonder how Homeland Security people watch things and just keep watching them and don't get colossally bored. Buses go by; one is blue, the other red with three white stripes and a lion on the side. A lady with no chin walks by.

What am I looking for?

I don't know.

I hope I'll know it when I see it.

A truck from Walmart goes by. Behind it is a truck from Crudup's with a picture of Caitlin in a cowgirl hat smiling at her dad like he's totally trustworthy.

Cars pull into Mabel's lot—a convertible with a beige interior, an electric green bug, a van covered, and I mean covered, in flowers. That's pretty great for the festival.

I'm watching the nail salon.

Watching the cars pull out of Mabel's.

The flowered van pulls out. I'd love to ride in that. It makes a right. I watch it go. I bolt up. On the back is . . .

PROUD TO BE AN AMERI

It pulls in behind Star Nails, and the van drives through the tall gate.

Okay, now I need help!

Twenty-Four

I look desperately around.

A big lady in a straw hat decorated with too many flowers walks slowly by.

I'm not asking her.

Now Dad pulls up, his face purple.

"You're in trouble, young lady."

I get in the car. "There's no time!" I tell him what I just saw, then I scream, "How do you call Homeland Security?"

Dad takes out his phone. "You call a grandmother." He parks in front of Mabel's.

One call to Winnie and she's on it like a police dispatcher. She calls Dad back. He puts her on speaker. "Brad is on his way. The sheriff is coming. Both of you, get to a safe place."

Dad looks at me.

"I'm fine," I say. And terrified. I keep that to myself.

We wait, we watch.

"What do you think is happening, Dad?"

"I don't know."

A big moving van pulls in front of the salon, blocking our view.

Dad gets out to look. "The driver is talking on the phone. I think he's lost."

I'm so upset, I feel like throwing up.

Dad looks at me. "Are you up for this?"

"I started it, Dad. I finish what I start."

Now I see the van heading out of the tall gate.

Where is the sheriff?

"Anna, wait here."

"I'm staying with you!"

The van is heading down the street!

Dad sighs deep. "Do not tell your mother."

Dad turns fast onto the street, gets two cars behind the van. He guns the car and gets in front of the van. Now he's going so slowly people are honking. Dad drives through the green light, makes a half turn, and stops, blocking the intersection. People lean on their horns.

Now we see Brad in a dark car driving toward us. Dad lifts a hand slightly. Brad sees the van. Dad guns the motor, like something is wrong with the engine.

If I wasn't sitting down, count on it, I'd faint.

Dad gets out of the car.

"Be careful, Dad!"

He lifts up the hood, shakes his head.

"Sorry!" he shouts to the cars who are stuck behind him, including the flower van. "I think my transmission died."

Now Brad pulls in right next to Dad, and the van swerves and rams right into Brad's car, just missing us. Brad jumps out like one of those guys in the movies. Another car comes behind the van—it can't move.

Brad's at the van now with his gun out. "Get out of the car," Brad says. "With your hands up."

The man in the van says something in another language.

Brad motions with his gun. The man understands that. He comes out with his hands up, and I swear this is the man I saw that day at the library!

Electricity is shooting through me.

I feel like I'm having a heart attack.

"Homeland Security!" Brad shouts. "Come out with your hands up!"

No one else comes out of the van.

Now the sheriff finally shows up. He puts handcuffs on the driver of the van, an Asian man who is shouting in his own language. Brad looks inside the flowered van. It looked so pretty just minutes before.

I close my eyes.

Be careful!

Brad steps back, holds his gun up.

"There's no one else," he says.

No one else!

More cars pull up, along with a big white van.

One pulls up behind Star Nails, another is on the side street, another parks right in front on Rose Street, one is across the street down from Mabel's. The agents signal to each other. Brad gets out, another man gets out, and they walk up to the front door in a way that says, *We're so not here to get manicures.*

Dad and I are across the street at Mabel's parking lot watching. We can't hear anything, but after several minutes, an agent brings out the Happy! guy, who is really not happy anymore.

He's shouting, "I'm legit. One hundred percent!"

People are stopping to look, and one of the agents shouts, "Move back, folks. Across the street, please. We've got to keep this area clear."

I lower my head and close my eyes, but Dad says, "Look."

I do, and now Brad and another man bring the women out who work there.

There are five of them—they look shocked and scared, but one looks up to the sunshine and she raises her hand and shouts, and another woman shouts, and now I see the lady who gave me the note, and I can tell that she's crying, and she's saying something and pointing behind her. I want to run up to her.

It's me, remember?

But I know I can't.

"Back away, please, folks, let these women have some privacy!"

A women agent is holding the hand of a nail lady, who looks shocked. They're looking at the sun and the sky and the trees and all the flowers like they haven't been outside in a while.

I don't understand what this means.

I don't know what they went through in there.

Dad puts his arm around me. "I'm proud of you, honey."

I keep looking and looking. The women from the

nail salon get in the big white van. It drives off. Then, one by one, the Homeland Security cars pull away until there's no one left except the people on the street wondering what happened.

But one thing is clear.

She's not there.

They didn't find her.

Dad squeezes my hand. "Anna, I think we should go—"

"No!"

I keep waiting and watching.

I'm glad the women are out, I'm so, so glad.

"Where is she?" I ask. "Where is she?"

It won't ever be right if they don't find her.

"Anna," Dad says, "so many things happened today that nobody expected. Don't start thinking you know how everything is going to end up."

Twenty-Five

We wait for news from Brad.

Hours pass. Winnie says, "Brad says things are shaping up."

What does that mean exactly?

I tell Dad I think Brad should be telling us something. "I mean, I started this, I didn't let it go, I waited, and I believed, I yelled at someone in the sheriff's office, and I think I deserve to know more than 'things are shaping up.' Shaping into what?"

Dad sighs and looks at Mim, who is getting ready to go to the hangar to check on the floats. "I know you don't normally hear this from me, Anna, but you need to be patient."

He's right. "Patient" is not a normal Dad concept.

Even Bean jerks his head when Dad utters the P word.

But patience isn't anything I've got right now.

I don't know how to wait anymore.

Right now it seems like all I know to do is worry.

But I know something that helps with that.

✿   ✿   ✿

"How you doing there, Zoe? I just came to see you, girl."
I rub her neck. "Is that okay?"

Zoe turns to look at me like she's glad I came.

I put my head against her side and sigh. I didn't
know you could be such good friends with a horse. I just
keep my head there.

"Are you good with this, girl?"

I can tell she's listening. I rub her side, pet her on
her hind leg, rub her on her face, and I don't know why,
but I just feel her strength coming at me. She knows I'm
hurting.

"Have you ever just felt nervous, you know, and you
can't get over it, and you don't know what to do? I don't
know how that works with horses, but with people,
we're supposed to think ourselves out of this stuff. But
the more I think the deeper I get."

I lift up some grass to her mouth, and she takes it.

"Does grass help with stress?"

Zoe stomps her back foot.

I hear, "Do you want to ride?" I turn to see Taylor.

"That's okay?"

"Of course."

Taylor puts a blanket on Zoe, then throws the saddle over her. "Up you go," she tells me.

I stick my foot in the stirrup and lift up like I do this all the time. I'd sure like to.

"Take her out, Anna."

I sit high above the ground holding the reins and grin.

"Go ahead," Taylor assures me.

I give a little tug, just a little, and we head out the stable door toward the ring.

"Take her on the trail," Taylor says. "She'll bring you back."

So we head to the tall trees, and Zoe knows where to go. "We're doing it, girl." Zoe's ears are a little forward, which means she's listening.

"Do you think we can trot a little?" I push my foot gently at her side. She picks up the pace. I'm bouncing up and down like an idiot, trying to remember how to go up and down with this. I find the rhythm.

Up and down, up and down.

Across the trail, past the thick green leaves, across a

little stream, past scurrying chipmunks and feathery ferns, along the path that this horse knows so well.

The sunshine is pouring through the trees, and it's like the path is lit somehow, and I feel something inside me, all the worry maybe, just give way to this ride, this horse.

"Whoa, girl."

She stops.

Whoa, Anna.

I close my eyes and just sit here, and I notice that my heart isn't racing; my mind isn't either.

I sit here with my friend.

I rub her neck.

And then it's time to head back. I touch the reins, and this huge horse turns just from that.

Just from a little touch!

"Let's go home, girl. Okay?"

I press my foot into her side so slightly, and we're heading back.

I duck at a low-hanging branch from a tree. I smile at a squirrel who climbs a tree.

I pat Zoe's neck. "Good girl, Zoe."

She trots out into the clearing like we do this all the time. Now I see Taylor's house and the riding ring.

"Let's look good getting there," I tell her, and I press my foot again and she speeds up to home.

I move with this horse—we're connected. I feel like we could race to California without stopping.

"Whoa, Zoe." She slows down.

Taylor is watching and smiling.

I bring her into the pen.

I get off.

"How was that?" Taylor asks.

"Better than anything."

I look at Zoe, who nuzzles me with her head.

"She thinks you have promise, Anna."

Zoe sticks her nose behind Taylor's straw hat and pushes it off.

Taylor laughs. "She likes my other hat better."

We walk to the stall.

I can't stop smiling.

"I have a question, Anna."

"What?"

She looks down. "I don't want to kill the moment, but do you think Burke might possibly . . . like me?"

"Yes."

"That was quick."

"It wasn't a hard question."

She rubs Zoe's mane. "Oh . . ."

"So, do you like him?"

Zoe turns around to look at Taylor. I wait.

"Possibly . . . I don't know . . ."

Zoe looks at me.

"You don't know?"

"Well, I mean . . ." Taylor coughs.

Being a preteen is so much easier—we get right down to it.

"Does he know you like him?"

Zoe looks at me like, *Of course not.* Taylor makes a noise.

I smile. "Do you want me to tell him you like him?"

"That, Anna, is the lamest idea!" She storms out.

Actually, I'm an experienced teller. I told Ronny Palto that Becca liked him and I told Lorenzo that Candy Turgin really liked him. I sang it, actually. I thought it would be fun news, but it wasn't.

"Candy Turgin!" Lorenzo shouted. "Just kill me now."

I look out the stall door. Taylor is outside pacing. "Someone needs to tell Burke," I say. She makes another noise. I go back to Zoe, who is easier to understand. I rub her down. Then I give her a hug—a big, long hug. I know hugging a horse might sound strange, but don't knock it until you've tried it.

There's a rustle behind me. Taylor again. "They've asked me to be the queen of the flowers for the parade. They want me to ride Zoe. Mim called me about it—the committee voted."

"You said yes, right?"

She grins. "There's a robe and headgear."

I laugh. "That's perfect."

"I was such a mess when I got here, Anna, I didn't even go to the parade . . . and now . . . well, I'm royalty."

Twenty-Six

The semi refrigerator trucks take over Rosemont for one day, delivering fresh flowers to the hangar.

"Now," Burke says, "it really gets crazy."

It wasn't crazy before?

My glue gun isn't working, and the blue carnations on the middle school jazz float keep falling off the giant musical note that is above the little stage where Ben and the band will be playing. Burke comes over with a brush and some glue. He shows me how to brush on the glue and then push a flower into it to make a pattern, one flower at a time.

"Brush and push over and over. You got it?" he asks.

"I've got it." I've been trying to figure out a way to bring up the subject of Taylor to see how he responds. Burke is fully float-focused, and it's hard to say, "So, I need more glue and blue carnations, and, by the way, that reminds me of Taylor."

Taylor is across the room working on the library bookworm. I can't see her, but I think Burke is looking over in her general direction, or maybe I'm making the whole thing up. Burke says more blue carnations are being delivered, which is the perfect moment for me to casually say, "Do you have a girlfriend?"

"What?"

I repeat the question.

"Not right now. No."

I look over to the corner, way over to where Taylor is working, and smile.

"What?" he says, not getting it.

"Oh nothing," I say, really staring at the corner now, pointing, actually, so he'll get the idea.

He doesn't. Siri and Ben carry the electric keyboard up onto the float. They plug it in. Siri plays a little as the Blues Mothers, two moms who support the band, walk by dressed in black.

Ben says, "Hi, Mrs. Wolsberger."

Jonathan Wolsberger, who plays guitar in the band, says his mother wears black in the house all day and dark sunglasses to really get into her role. The entire Wolsberger family can't wait for the parade to be over.

Siri plays some more.

I look around this hangar at all the volunteers who've come to help, at all the flowers, the colors, the different floats, at the smiles and the focus of the people, at the old people leaning on their canes, at the young kids so excited to be doing anything, at the ladders, at this community of people who meet every year to celebrate the best this town has got.

Harvey Mutt himself is on his plumbing float, gluing carnations on the waving chipmunk.

"Hey, Harvey," an old guy says. "You should have a toilet in the middle so people can relate."

Harvey Mutt laughs. "I got something better, Buck."

The animal rescue float has faces of dogs and cats, and a dog lifting its leg by a big tree with birds looking down.

The Small Business Association has a sign that says, WE'RE IN THIS TOGETHER, and an excellent gazebo.

And Chip Hoover Chevrolet has a car on their float that's dripping with flowers. They're having a problem with their inflatable dancing man balloon—the flowers keep falling off it—but they do have a huge picture of Chip Hoover that's being filled in with carnations.

It's hard to not feel happy here.

I touch the yellow scrunchie. Except I don't know

how to stay happy, and I don't think I should.

I think about the girl in the van, and every bit of happiness in me runs out.

How can the world have so many different parts to it?

I see Dad walking toward me. "Brad wants to see us."

"What did he say?"

"Just that he wants to see us."

That doesn't sound good . . .

Dad and I head out the door.

✿   ✿   ✿

I look at the basket of peach muffins in the kitchen.

Mim pours coffee.

I'm trying to read Brad's face. Winnie says to him, "You look tired."

"I'm all right." He takes a sip of coffee. "Let me start with what we know for sure. It looks as though Mr. Deng of Star Nails was forcing women to work at his nail salon for little, possibly no, money. They were the equivalent of slaves. And three other nail salons were involved in this practice. We raided them all."

I don't move.

"This kind of activity is more common than people understand," Brad continues. "The women at Star Nails were working against their will. They had no free-dom. They'd been brought to this country under false pretenses—promised they'd have good jobs, nice houses. Instead, they entered a nightmare. They've been beaten, threatened, their families have been threatened, and some of them are afraid to testify against the people who did this. That's what happens in these cases. It's a terrible, terrible cycle."

I look at my nails—most of the polish is gone, but I want to rub it all off, all of it.

"Now the woman who gave you the note, Anna, she is the mother of the girl you saw. She told us her story. She and her daughter had been brought here with big promises of a good job, good schools . . ."

I'm having trouble sitting still.

"She said Mr. Deng would often separate her from her daughter to make sure the mother did what he want-ed her to do."

"What did the note say?"

"It said it all. She and her daughter were being held against their will and they needed help."

I'm trying to take this all in. "What about the lady in the van?"

"We're trying to understand her involvement."

"Where's the girl?" I ask quietly.

Brad taps his fingers on his knee. "We're working on that."

"It's not done till you find her," I remind him.

"I know."

The doorbell rings.

I need to move. "I'll get it."

I open the door.

"Oh wow," I say.

The room starts spinning.

That's the last thing I remember.

Twenty-Seven

"Anna!"

That's me. I open my eyes.

"Honey, are you all right?" That's my mom asking. She's kneeling by my side.

What's she doing here?

Now I remember—when I opened the door, she was standing there.

"Hi, Mom."

Brad and Mim stand over me. We're gathered in Mim's hall right by the NO WHINING sign.

"What is going on here?" Mom demands.

"Take it easy, Sarah." That's Dad. It's never good when he tells her to take it easy.

"I resent your tone, Brian!"

I wave my hand pitifully. "How about the kid on the floor?"

"Can you sit up?" Dad asks me.

"Maybe."

He helps me do that.

"Don't let the blood rush too fast to her head!" Mom shouts.

Or rush too slow. I shake my head to get the blood flowing.

Dad looks at me. "Lots going on here, huh, kiddo? Did things get a little too much?"

"Maybe."

I feel like I woke up in a new land—well, not exactly new, my parents are still fighting.

"I'm okay, Mom." She's not convinced. I look at Bean. He comes over to check.

Dad gives me water. Brad kneels down.

"What I want to tell you, Anna, is that the biggest break in this case was your finding the mother. She had one picture of her daughter and she gave that to us." He opens his phone and shows it to me. "Is this the girl you saw?"

The girl is smiling in this picture, not scared. Her eyes just seem big and wondering, not lost and frightened. She's wearing a small necklace. Everything about her is delicate. But I can see she's strong.

"That's her," I whisper.

"Her name," Brad says, "is Kim Su."

"Kim Su," I repeat. I try to memorize her face. Brad looks square at me. "We're on this, and we wouldn't be if it wasn't for you." He pats my shoulder. "Keep doing what you're doing."

I laugh. "You mean faint again?"

"Maybe not that." He smiles like a superhero.

And Brad is out the door.

No cape, but still . . .

✿ ✿ ✿

Dad takes Mim to the hangar to encourage the workers. The parade is tomorrow and Mom is staying till Sunday to watch me. She didn't put it that way, but a kid knows these things.

Flower Madness takes over Rosemont.

Everywhere in town there's beauty and color.

I keep trying not to think about Kim Su, but she's all I can think about.

I need an off button on my brain.

Maybe she was taken in a van to Canada.

Maybe she's sick and can't get medicine.

Maybe she's so scared she can't talk.

Maybe she's given up hope.

Bean, the hope dog, comes over, but I'm not feeling much hope anywhere.

He drops the ball and looks at me like, *Pick it up. Do something.*

He nudges it forward.

"I can't right now, Bean."

I sit down and try to draw Kim Su's face—what I saw of it on Brad's phone.

This doesn't look anything like her.

Right then, I get the idea.

It's such a gargantuan idea, I already know it can't work.

There's not enough time.

Too many people would have to be involved.

No one can do this.

But I write down everything that comes to me.

I fill four sheets of paper.

It's crazy.

I run out the door and head to the hangar to find Ben and Siri.

❀   ❀   ❀

I run over to the middle school jazz band float. Ben is sticking yellow daisies on a half moon that hangs over the big musical note that is filled in with lentils.

"I have an idea!" I shout. "We have to talk now!"

Every kid at work stops and looks at me. Caitlin puts down her trumpet. Siri puts down her glue brush.

I add, "I need to mention that the whole thing is impossible!"

Ben thinks about this. "I'm in."

"Me, too." That's Caitlin.

Siri says, "Don't you think we should know what this is first?"

We head outside, sit on a picnic bench under a flowering pink tree.

I draw what I see.

"Okay, and everybody's got to do it . . . that's how this works."

They study what I drew.

Ben takes my pencil. "What if it looked like this?" He draws. I'm a better artist, but he's got a better idea.

"That's good, Ben."

Siri says, "But we don't have enough time."

"I know."

"And we don't have the money to do this."

She's right again.

Caitlin is studying the paper like it's going to be on a

test. Ben says to me, "Don't you have to get permission from the big guys?"

I'm pretty sure the answer is yes. I take out Brad's card and call him. He answers. I explain.

Brad is quiet at first. "This is a little unusual, Anna." No kidding.

"All right," he says. "You'll have it in a minute."

I hold my phone, waiting. Then the buzz. I've got it.

"Thank you, Brad."

Now Caitlin comes over waving the paper showing The Big Idea. "We need to tell my father."

Whoa! I don't think so.

Ben says, "I don't think your dad would really—"

"Yes he would."

Okay, I might as well put this in a shredder.

"He would," Caitlin insists. She grabs my arm. "Come on, Anna. We're going to tell him."

"Uh . . ." I look at Ben, who makes a *good luck* face. "Caitlin, really, I don't think your dad even likes me."

She folds her arms. "It's not about liking people, it's about getting the job done, doing the deal. My father taught me all about that."

I look desperately at Ben and Siri. "Maybe we should all go?"

They shake their cowards' heads and step back.

"Come on, Anna! Daddy is a busy man!"

❀ ❀ ❀

Coleman Crudup is sitting in his office, although it should probably be called an apartment, it's that big.

It has a long table with eight leather chairs and fat rugs on the floors and photos of Coleman Crudup himself doing outdoor adventurer things—holding up a huge fish he caught, standing by a dead deer that he shot. There's one of him on top of a mountain with his hands on his hips like he personally owns the land. There are lots of pictures of him smiling too big and shaking hands with people, and one, and this is the one I'm focusing on, of him riding a camel in the desert.

At least he didn't shoot it.

He is sitting at his desk, which is so big it could belong to a giant who keeps a woolly mammoth as a pet. A few minutes ago, Caitlin and I just burst in, and she announced, "Daddy, we totally, and I mean totally, need you to listen to something. It's huge, Daddy. Huge."

There's this awful silence in the room as Coleman Crudup looks at me. I go back to studying the dead deer photo.

"You ever shot a deer?" His voice is big and bounces off the dark wood wall.

"No, sir. I've waved at them. That's it."

"You gotta get out there in this world, make your presence known."

I feel it's best to nod.

"You were a strawberry," he says.

"No, sir, a petunia. You wanted to hire me to be a strawberry."

"A world-class strawberry."

I nod and don't mention the fifty dollars.

"Why didn't you want to work for me?"

Caitlin steps forward. "Daddy, we're not here to talk about that."

Coleman Crudup leans back in his huge chair and studies me. "How's the petunia thing going?"

"Pretty well, except for the hat."

"Always something."

"Right, sir."

I shouldn't be here.

Caitlin tosses her blonde hair. "Daddy, Anna has an awesome idea she wants to talk to you about."

"Uh, no, I don't think I should be the one to—"

"It costs money, Daddy, but it's important and you can lead the way."

That isn't part of the idea. He leans forward in his big leather chair.

I smile.

He doesn't.

"You, Daddy, can show the world what you really care about."

He sits up a little straighter.

"And I care about this so much, Daddy, that if we can't do it, I just don't think I can handle it. You can do anything. I know you can." Caitlin walks over and puts her hand on her father's arm. She nods to me. I wasn't expecting this. It wasn't my idea to come and see her father.

But I say, "Well, sir, probably only someone like you could make this happen and it needs to happen fast."

"Superfast, Daddy."

"And," I add, "we need to start right away."

"Time is running out, Daddy." Caitlin takes a huge breath. "This is what I want for my birthday."

He looks at her. "I thought you wanted a trip to Paris."

Nice present.

She shakes her blonde hair. "I want this."

He stands up. "Will someone please tell me what this is!"

So I tell him.

I take out my pages of notes and lay them out on his humongous desk.

I hold up my hand with the yellow scrunchie around my wrist. Caitlin holds hers up, too.

And I'm telling you now, I wouldn't believe it if I hadn't seen it myself. Because the minute I explain the whole, impossible thing and show him the photograph, Coleman Crudup actually gets kind of choked up.

He looks at Caitlin and says, "God. That's brilliant."

Not impossible.

Not too big.

Not too crazy.

Brilliant.

"Of course we'll do it." He slaps the desk, and picks up my last piece of paper. "I suggest one change."

"Yes, sir."

"It needs to happen all at once. A trumpet needs to sound." He looks at Caitlin, who beams. "And then you do it."

"That's good, Daddy."

"That totally works, sir."

And the next thing he says is even crazier: "And I'm going to pay for the whole thing!"

"Oh, Daddy!"

It just seems right: I take off the yellow scrunchie from my wrist and hand it to him.

"I've got another one at home, sir. I'm sorry about the spaghetti sauce stain. I think you can wash it off."

Coleman Crudup looks at the scrunchie. Caitlin puts it on his wrist. "Thank you, Anna."

Now, I didn't learn deal-making from my dad, but one thing he always taught me.

Know when it's time to leave.

I shout, "Thank *you*, sir." I turn to go, take a last look at the photo of Coleman Crudup and the dead deer.

I'm outta here.

Twenty-Eight

A zillion things to do and not enough people to do them, but somehow they're getting done.

Dr. Gudrey puts special composite horseshoes on Zoe so she won't slip on the pavement along the parade route.

Taylor is getting into her role as the queen of the flowers, maybe a little too much.

She's wearing a purple robe and a gold crown, and she's riding around the ring on Zoe, who has a wreath of flowers over her neck. They're going to lead the parade. But some rulers want it all.

"I'll need a scepter of authority, of course, and a small floral entourage to do my bidding . . ." Taylor looks at me.

I'm so much more than part of an entourage!

"We'll find a scepter," Dad assures her.

I think you're creating a monster here!

Six marching bands come into town.

The bands are practicing on the Rosemont High School football field, but no band is as cool as MSB, the Middle School Blues. They're wearing blue jackets and black shirts, crazy shorts, and matching dark sunglasses.

The Blues are ready to rock hearts.

Caitlin is practicing her big trumpet call.

Merv is practicing his cowboy rope tricks, shouting "Yeee-haaa!" a lot.

Cars drive down the street covered with flowers.

Out come hats with feathers and flowers, sequined outfits, glittery tops.

Ben hands me a pair of dark sunglasses. "You're one of us, Anna, even though you have to watch the daisies."

Burke keeps bringing more flowers to decorate Taylor's crown. I try to get things going between them, but twelve-year-olds are much better conversationalists than older teenagers.

Believe me, I've done what I can.

Mim sits at home "resting" for as long as she can stand it. Finally she wears Dad down and he drives her to the hangar. I go, too.

You can't believe how good the floats look.

Mim takes the microphone and stands in the middle of it all. "All right, we've got more work than a sane person can even think about, but anyone volunteering for this isn't fully sane." That gets a laugh. "So, from my heart, from the mayor of Rosemont, from every person in this town, I want to thank you all for being here and wanting to make something uniquely beautiful that's going to delight so many people." She looks around grinning. "And, oh, you've done it! It's gorgeous. Thank you, thank you!"

A little girl in a yellow shirt runs up to her. "You're welcome!"

Mim pulls the kid up with her. "This is what it's about. I love you all."

A cheer goes up.

All night long we work—not exactly all night, but way late. Still, I do think it's fair to say that Coleman Crudup's people who were assigned to Get the Big Thing Done didn't sleep at all.

❀   ❀   ❀

"Good morning, entourage." It's Taylor, our supreme ruler.

I'm back in the petunia suit, surrounded by a cactus,

a sneezing yellow rose, and ten little daisies who aren't getting along. Roderick von Push, age six, is a dandelion.

"What's my motivation?" he says to Taylor.

"You're a weed, Roderick. You spread."

Roderick's not sure about the spreading.

"My public awaits," Taylor says, and raises her scepter. "You may rise."

"I'm already standing!" That's Roderick.

"Places," Dad says.

And Taylor and her entourage walk to the front of the parade line, past the miniature cars, the flower-covered bikes, the skateboarders, the seven floats, each one so different. A few of them, like the MSB float, have some bald spots, but that's okay, life isn't perfect.

Past the marching bands and the cactus mobile, driven by an old guy who looks like a cactus, past horses and veterans in convertibles, past majorettes and minor-ettes, and as we walk past the MSB float, the whole band stands up and shouts, "Yeah!"

I've got on my serious jazz MSB dark sunglasses be-cause I am part of that group and proud to be a cool petunia.

I do a grooving petunia move, and the little daisies follow me the best they can.

The band nods their heads and says, "Yeah," again.

"Dandelions don't dance," Roderick tells me.

Whatever.

All the while Taylor is waving, and people are waving back.

Burke comes up to her with this dumb expression on his face, and he escorts her to Zoe like she can't get on a horse by herself.

"You may call me 'Your Majesty,'" Taylor tells me as she walks by.

I cough. Maybe not.

So, here we are.

There's no more time.

I hope it got done.

I hope, I hope, I hope . . .

Twenty-Nine

A drumroll.

Slowly the parade begins.

Zoe shakes her head and walks forward.

Taylor adjusts her head mic.

"Ladies, gentlemen, children, and all manner of distinctive creatures," she announces as her voice booms from amplifiers across the parade route. "Welcome to the Parade of Flowers. We have a special theme today. In the middle of all this beauty, we are raising a banner of hope."

That's Burke's and Dad's cue. They're right behind me. I turn around to see.

They raise a banner high.

It says, OGM.

A teenage girl shouts, "Shouldn't that be OMG?"

"Absolutely not." Taylor lifts her scepter.

Caitlin Crudup blows her trumpet good and loud.

And banners on all the floats roll down like sails on tall ships. Those banners read,

ONE GIRL MATTERS

Now, thanks to Brad, the smiling picture of Kim Su is raised by marchers. Kids dressed like flowers, and one small, irritable weed, pass out the HAVE YOU SEEN HER? cards.

Did I mention that everyone in the parade has a yellow scrunchie on their wrist? Drums roll again.

Another trumpet blast, not as strong as the first one, but people get the idea.

Me, I'm dancing.

I was made to be a petunia.

I suppose Taylor was always meant to be the queen of the flowers. She plays it as if she was born for the role.

"Have you any wishes?" she shouts down to the people. "Is everything going well for you in the kingdom? Have you met my little flowers and our weed?"

"I spread," Roderick explains.

I moonwalk, and the crowd loves it. All the hours

Lorenzo and I practiced to get this right are paying off now. I throw in a break-dance move.

The crowd loves that, too.

Petunias can do anything.

"Thank you all for coming," Taylor tells the crowd. "I love being out among the people."

She jumps off Zoe to shake hands. She orders us flowers around, but not too much.

I nod to the daisies, and they skip off in a perfect line to weave in and out of the floats. I walk alongside them.

"Wave. Be adorable."

They do this.

Roderick looks disgusted.

"You're a weed," I tell him. "Look tough."

He puts his extreme weed face on.

"That's what I'm talking about, Roderick. Who is going to mess with you?"

I can hear the Middle School Blues start up.

I've marched in parades before, but nothing like this.

If I felt any more energy, I swear, I could fly!

Dad and Burke are marching in front of the MSB band holding the ONE GIRL MATTERS banner high. The little flowers are everywhere, passing out OGM buttons.

"Boys matter, too," Roderick tells people.

I weave in and out with the daisies and our one irritable weed. All the daisies stop and wave at the waving chipmunk on Harvey Mutt Plumbing, Ltd. Lots of people in the crowd are laughing as Harvey Mutt raises a plunger and shouts, "Life is good!"

I zigzag with the daisies, and we get to the end of the parade. Coleman Crudup's float seems to break all the rules. His name is too big, his music is too loud, but his ONE GIRL MATTERS sign is ten feet tall, bigger than his name even, and that is something.

Of course under that is written, "Brought to you by Crudup Country Markets."

Coleman Crudup walks alongside his float shaking hands and passing out yellow scrunchies.

The daisies and I dance around him.

Back to the front now. "Stay adorable!" I shout as we move alongside the bookworm float. The head of the worm moves a little—the kids love it. Mim and Winnie are under a reading tree, waving.

Waving is a big part of being in a parade.

Merv rides on a horse and does his rope tricks from high in the saddle.

Volunteers walk along the parade route wearing OGM buttons.

Somebody see her, please.

Somebody remember.

Roderick runs up to me. "They want you on the middle school float, Anna."

I look behind me and Ben is motioning to me. I run over. He helps me onto the float.

"Come on, Anna. We need you to sing." He hands me a mic.

"No. I can't."

"Of course you can," Siri says.

"I haven't practiced for—"

Mr. Cool doesn't wait for permission. He grins at me. "Give it all you got."

He snaps his fingers. The band gets ready. Mr. Cool says, "One, two, three, four . . ." The band breaks into Ben's song. Mr. Cool nods at me. "Take it."

Did anyone notice I'm in a petunia suit?

But I adjust my sunglasses, hold the mic, and sing . . .

Tell me how you're doing,

I really want to know.

Are you feeling happy
Or are you feeling low?

Tell me if it's bad for you.
Tell me what you need.

I throw back my head . . .

I'm your friend.
And you can count on me.
Oh yeah . . .

"Yeah, girl," Mr. Cool says.
I'm strutting now.

You can count on me!

The band is doing it. Ben is grinning at me.
I get ready for the second verse.
I'm singing . . .

People make us crazy.
People turn away . . .

Tell Me

Caitlin comes in so true with her trumpet.

I grin at her.

That is good.

The beat is strong,

I'm dancing to the song.

I twirl around, hands in the air.

And this petunia grooves across the stage.

The band nods.

Tell me how you're doing,

I really want to know.

Are you feeling happy

Or are you feeling low?

Caitlin's trumpet rises.

Tell me if it's bad for you.

Tell me what you need.

I'm your friend.

Ben sings, "Yes, she is."

I'm your friend,

Oh yeah.

I throw my petunia arms out.

I'm going for the big finish. . . .

You . . .

Can . . .

Count . . .

Onnnnnnn . . .

Ben does a great drum lick. Caitlin blares her horn.
I throw back my head and belt out,

Meeeeeeee!

I have never held a note this long, I swear.

✿　✿　✿

People are applauding, and Mr. Cool nods, which is
major praise. Ben twirls his drum sticks in the air. It's
just one of those official best moments you want to last
forever.

Mr. Cool tells me to take a bow, and he tells the
band to stand up.

We wave at the people as petals are thrown into the
streets of Rosemont.

Mom waves at me from the crowd, dabbing her eyes.

And suddenly I understand something about what to do when bad things come. You don't hide, you don't look away; you get right up on them, you take the reins and you ride.

Or sing.

Or whatever it is you know how to do.

And I swear, this experience is even better than being a singing radish, but all good things have to come to an end.

Roderick von Push runs up to the float and shouts, "Anna, the flowers are running off!"

I hand Mr. Cool the mic, jump off the float, and try to collect the daisies, which isn't easy in this outfit.

Taylor grabs two giggling daisies and the rose, Roderick screams at the tiny cactus, and Dad and Burke help us get the kids in line.

"That was some performance," Dad tells me. "I've never heard you better."

"It's Ben's song," I say.

"It's everybody's song now, Anna."

I look at Kim Su's smiling picture hanging down from all these banners.

This has to be enough to find her.

Has to be.

Have you seen her?
Please say yes.
She's my friend.

      ✿   ✿   ✿

All day long and into the night, people talk about the girl with the baby animal eyes.

The floats are awarded the trophies—the bookworm takes first prize, the middle school float gets "Best First Effort." Harvey Mutt Plumbing, Ltd., gets "Most Beautiful," and he makes a big speech about beauty and plumbing, and at the end he raises his trophy in one hand and his plunger in the other.

Coleman Crudup doesn't get a trophy, but I tell him, "You get the yellow scrunchie award, sir. It's only being given once and won't be given again. You totally deserve it."

He snaps the scrunchie on his wrist and says he'll take it.

"And there's prize money, sir." I open my velcro wrist wallet and hand him the fifty-dollar bill he gave me at the library. "I know that's not a lot to you, but . . ."

He takes the money. "Any time you want to work for

me, Anna McConnell, you give me a call. Any time, and that includes after college."

"Thank you, sir."

We've done everything we know to do, and that's such a good feeling.

Now we wait.

Thirty

I've gotten better at so many things since I've come to Rosemont.

But not waiting.

I've thrown the ball to Bean nineteen times, which is the number of years my parents have been married. I'm doing this and looking in Mim's big kitchen window, which isn't easy, but the good news is my parents are in there talking. A few times the talking moves to fighting and Dad stands up and starts pointing his finger, and Mom stands up and points hers right back, but once Dad grabs her hand and that settles things down, and once Mom starts to cry, which I feel is a good move because it causes Dad to put his arm around her.

"Bean, I'm pretty sure they might need me in there. What do you think?"

Bean drops the ball at my feet, which means *throw again*.

So I throw again, and he jumps up and gets it. I throw it a grand total of forty-seven times, and I'm hoping that my parents will be married at least that many years. I was going for fifty, but my shoulder gives out. Bean doesn't stand for wimpy throws; you've got to put your whole heart into it.

It's funny how Mim's racing heart and looking for Kim Su has brought our family back together.

I'm throwing the ball to Bean by the split-rail fence. Taylor rides up on Zoe, not looking too good.

"Hi."

She nods.

"Are you okay, Taylor?"

She takes a deep sigh. "Partially."

I put the ball down, climb over the fence, walk to them. "What's wrong?" I get close and Zoe walks to me, puts her head close to my shoulder.

"I have to visit my dad and his wife."

"Oh . . ."

"She's having a surprise birthday for him." Taylor winces. "It's a costume party."

"You could go as the queen of the flowers."

"You're only twelve, Anna. How did you get so smart?"

"I don't know. I just keep going."

✿ ✿ ✿

Dad and I walk Mom out to her car. She has to be at work tomorrow. Dad is staying a few more days.

Mom looks at Dad. "Well, Brian, I—"

Dad takes her in his arms. Bean wags his tail.

Way to go, Dad.

Mom looks at me. "What do I say to you?"

I smile. "You'll get me a horse?"

She messes up my hair. "You can visit the horse."

Dad starts giving her directions to get back—but they're Dad directions, which include all the ways to go if things go wrong.

Mom climbs in the car, turns on the GPS. "I'll see you in a few days."

Major waving. After the parade, we know how to wave in this family.

So many people are leaving.

Ben is going to music camp.

Taylor is going to her father's birthday party.

Lorenzo wants to know when I'm coming back.

All of Rosemont is cleaning up from the parade. Flowers don't last long.

I guess you don't always get the things you work and hope for.

I touch my yellow scrunchie.

Come on!

✿　✿　✿

Mim's doorbell rings.

She shouts, "It's Homeland Security."

I run out. Brad and Winnie are in the living room.

Brad says, "A tip came in from a Vietnamese businessman two towns away. He's sure he's seen Kim Su."

I put my hand over the scrunchie and close my eyes.

Keep hoping!

Things are happening!

He smiles. "Just hang tough, Anna."

I'm getting seriously sick of hanging tough.

But it's the only way, especially for a former petunia.

Thirty-One

I got lost once at a carnival. I was four and I couldn't find my parents. There was so much noise and crazy rides and screaming and I felt like I was stuck in the scariest place and I couldn't get out.

Finally, I saw my mother running up to me shouting, "Anna! I'm here! I've been looking for you everywhere!"

Every lost girl needs to know someone is trying to find her.

Have you seen her?

Suddenly, I feel kind of lost in the big, bad world.

I push back and forth on the glider in Mim's garden, thinking about people in slavery and kids in vans who are hidden. My mouth feels dry, I just can't imagine . . .

One girl matters, I tell myself.

One kid.

I see Mim rushing out the back door, her face lit up with sunshine. "They found her!"

I sit there frozen.

What did she say?

"They found her, Anna."

Something shoots through me, I can't speak.

Winnie comes out talking about a Vietnamese store owner who saw Kim Su's picture and realized she might be staying in a house on his street. He called the number on our card. Then Brad got the local police to surround that place.

Dad comes out, talking on the phone: "Yes, yes, I'll tell her." He grins at me. "Two men and a woman have been arrested."

They found her.

They found her!

I leap up.

"Brad says the two men and the lady are in custody."

I nod. That's all I can do.

"How is the girl?" Dad asks.

"Safe now," Winnie says. "They've got her, and they're bringing her mother to the station."

And all the days of hoping and wondering what to do, all the pictures I had in my head, all the fear, all the anger at those awful people, all the worry, and the sadness—it is all being painted over in another color.

I'm not sure if there is an official hope color.

"Can I see her?" I ask.

"Oh, honey, I don't think so," Mim says.

"She's going to need some time to heal," Dad begins, "and—"

"But can we ask somebody?"

Winnie shakes her head. "I think she'll need to be with professionals who handle these kinds of things. They'll understand how to help her."

How do I let them know?

It's not just anyone asking.

I'm her friend!

❖　❖　❖

Four nail salons were shut down because of human trafficking. One in Iowa, three in Virginia. Brad said there could be more.

"It's because of you, Anna," Brad tells me.

"Not just me . . ."

"None of this would have happened without you."

"Or you," I mention.

Kim Su and her mother are in a safe place with people who are trained to help them. I'm not trained that way, but I know what it means to be a good friend.

"Can I meet her?" I ask Brad.

He looks at me. "I don't know, Anna, but I'll check."

"She'll need to see another kid, you know!"

❀ ❀ ❀

Everything is ready in the backyard—the table is set, the flowers in vases. I even gave Bean a bath—he actually changed color. Nothing could help his ball.

Winnie is here.

Dad headed back to Philadelphia.

We were told not to have too many people.

We're waiting.

The strawberry shortcake is on the counter. I already whipped the cream.

"Maybe something happened and they can't come," I say.

"They're coming," Winnie insists.

We wait some more.

I'm trying to picture what it's going to be like. I look out the window and see a dark car pull up outside. Brad and a woman get out, then the back door opens and an Asian man climbs out.

Now I see her. She's looking out the window of the car.

I start to run outside, but Mim holds me back. "Give her some space. She's been through a lot."

I watch Kim Su walk up our steps holding her mother's hand. They both look down. They are both pretty. The Asian man is talking to them and pointing to the flowers in Mim's front yard. I thought about turning on the bubble maker, but that was probably too much.

I want this to be just right.

They are at our door now. The bell rings.

Mim opens the door. Brad says, "Sorry we're late." He smiles at me. "Anna, I want you to meet Kim Su and her mother, Mai."

You can picture something in your head a thousand times, but it's never like when it really happens.

The mother takes both my hands in hers, lowers her eyes, and whispers something I don't understand. "Miss Anna," the Asian man says gently, "this mother thanks you from her heart."

"You're welcome," I whisper.

The Asian man speaks to the girl in her language. She comes forward and gives me a flower. She looks at me now with her baby animal eyes. The man slowly says, "Thank you, my friend."

The girl looks down and tries. "Tank you . . ."

"My friend," the man says slowly.

Very slowly she says, "My fend."

I nod and touch my heart. Kim Su nods and touches her heart and then her mother does, too.

Bean comes over with his ball, wagging his tail.

"Not now, Bean." But Bean speaks heart, being a hope dog. He trots to Kim Su, sits, and puts the ball at her feet, waiting.

"It's pretty dirty," I tell her, "but it means he likes you."

The Asian man translates this, and she smiles. She picks up the ball and Bean gets excited. We head out back. I show her how to throw the ball to Bean.

She is seriously good at this, and she laughs as Bean catches each throw. She throws it between her legs. Bean loves that, scoops it up and brings it back to her. Kim Su doesn't get tired of this. I think it's good for her to play.

Things are going really well, but then she runs to the door, and her mother and the man take her outside to the car.

I wonder if I can say good-bye.

I hope I didn't do the wrong thing, I hope I didn't scare her.

Brad says, "She hasn't been around people like this.

She needs to take little steps to feel safe. Does that make sense?"

I know about little steps.

I try not to go to the window to see if she's okay, and eventually she and her mother come back inside.

The strawberry shortcake helps everything. I can tell she's never had strawberry shortcake before, and actually, no one really has had strawberry shortcake until they've had Mim's.

"I have a present for you," I tell her, and the Asian man repeats that.

I get out a bouquet of flowers that I picked from Mim's garden—it's the best bouquet I've ever put together, with curling ribbons on the vase.

"Ohhhh!" she says.

I know what that means!

Then I hand her a box. She opens it and says, "Oh!" again as she pulls out the little bracelet with the pink heart that I picked out myself.

I help her put it on. She touches her heart and I touch mine. Then very gently I walk closer and I give Kim Su a hug. At first she jumps, but I just keep hugging her and then she hugs me back.

Her mother bows to me and I bow back, and Kim Su bows and I bow back, then the translator starts bowing to everyone and Brad gets into it, and Mim starts now and Winnie is bowing, too. I forget who I've bowed to, so I bow to Bean, who doesn't bow but he does wag his tail.

And after that the party is over.

I sit down on the front steps as the car pulls away.

It's official. This is the best day of my life.

Thirty-Two

I walk to the birdhouse, to the path that leads around Mim's garden. The flowers are bigger than when I got here.

I'm bigger, too.

I've ridden a horse.

I've helped capture bad guys.

I might have had something to do with my parents getting back together.

I've been a singing petunia.

I hope there's an essay in eighth grade about how I spent my summer vacation, because I don't want all this material to go to waste.

But now I have to go home.

It's not easy to say good-bye to people when you've shared major life moments.

Winnie's eyes get red when I hug her.

"I'll be back," I tell her.

I want to transport Siri and Ben to Philadelphia.

Ben is leaving for camp in one hour. He hands me a CD of the middle school jazz band. Siri says, "I think you should live here, Anna."

Part of me does, too.

"I'll be back, you guys."

Now for the really hard good-bye . . .

❋ ❋ ❋

"You can brush her down if you want to."

I take the curry comb from Taylor and move it in the circle motions. I don't want to leave this horse.

Zoe turns to look at me.

"I guess you know I have to go. I don't live here officially."

Zoe knows this.

Taylor peeks back in. "For a twelve-year-old, Anna, you're beyond okay."

"Thanks."

"Actually, I think you're kind of ageless."

"And I think you're the coolest friend to share your horse."

Taylor leans against the stall door. "That was pretty awesome of me."

I give Taylor a hug. She says, "I'll leave you two alone."

I stand there brushing Zoe.

I look at her. *So, what are you about?*

I think you like the fact that you're strong and you can give people a ride.

I think you like to go fast.

I think you know about loving.

You can tell when somebody's hurting.

I think you care about that because of what happened to you.

She moves her great horse head across my shoulder. I feel her strength and her heart as close as anything.

I wonder—if you'd just had an easy horse life, would you care this much?

❁ ❁ ❁

Mim and I stand at the train station.

"I'm going to miss having you around, Anna."

"I'm going to miss being around. I'll be back."

"You'd better."

I smile. "How 'bout next week?"

"I'd love it, but I'm not sure how your parents would feel about it."

Speaking of my parents . . .

Mim is probably the wisest person I know, so I ask, "Do you have any advice for me about Mom and Dad and everything?"

She thinks about that. "Well, it seems to me, when people are going through a hard, confusing time, they need a little encouragement, so if you can step up and encourage your parents, I think that would help them and you."

I'm not sure how it will help me, and I tell her that.

"It'll help you focus on the best parts of them," she explains.

"I'll try, Mim."

"Something tells me you'll do more than try." She hugs me hard and I hang on. The train is boarding. "Off you go now."

Mim touches her heart and I touch mine.

Thirty-Three

"Thank God you're back, kid." Fred Dimsdale grabs my hand. "Your replacement . . ." he shakes his head. "It was painful to watch. He was clueless, no connection with the people, no understanding of the heart of a cranberry."

I'm in the cranberry suit. "I won't let you down, sir."

Lorenzo adjusts his I'M WITH THE CRANBERRY button and grins as the big music starts up. Dance music.

And I am a dancing cranberry!

"Remember, Anna. The drama coach for the high school is here to see us. I told her we were good enough to go to their after-school program."

I nod. We are good enough.

We run out of the store, rocking, clapping, shouting, "Yes!"

Clapping to the beat.

One, two, three, four . . .

Lorenzo struts over, holding the mic.

I dance around him like we practiced.

Lorenzo shouts to the crowd, "Have you had your antioxidants today?"

I pause, cup my ear, listening to hear if the people say yes.

Nobody's shouting. They will.

"Have you?"

The crowd shouts back.

One, two, three, four . . .

A woman runs up, puts her arm around me and motions to a man. "Take my picture with the raisin, Herb."

"Actually, ma'am, I'm not a—"

"She's a cranberry, lady!" That's my dad.

"Well, excuse me!" the woman says.

Small Dumb Move, Dad. I put my hand up for Dad to cool down.

Dad starts laughing. I put my arm around the lady and pose.

Herb moves into place with his camera. "Everybody smile."

Yeah, I know about smiling.

They get my extreme cranberry grin.

Click.

I give her a coupon.

"You look like a raisin," she says, and glares at Dad.

Fred Dimsdale groans at this news. Raisins are his big competition.

Thinking quickly, Lorenzo shouts, "But can a raisin do this?"

He points to me and I do a cartwheel, which isn't easy in a cranberry suit. We've added a lot of new moves. I don't land too well, but everyone's applauding.

People are coming over to dance with me and get their pictures taken.

Fred Dimsdale is happy.

Dad is as happy.

The drama coach from the high school is smiling. This is good.

Mom walks up carrying shopping bags. Dad looks less than happy that she's bought so much stuff.

Let it go, Dad.

I run over, put my arm around him.

He laughs again

I wish Mim were here. But I picture her in her garden. I picture her heart getting stronger.

I wish Kim Su were here. I have a feeling that one of these days she could be a very good dancing cranberry, and I don't say that about just anybody.

I look out at the faces and, for a minute, I don't just see a crowd, I see people, real people, and I wonder where they're happy and where they hurt and what things do they keep down inside and what do they love most. And being in the cranberry suit helps me look at them in a different way.

Some kids run up to me, and we jump up and down on the little stage in front of the Wide World of Cranberries store.

Two of them giggle and run back to their parents, but a small boy with sad eyes looks up at me and quietly says, "My dog is sick."

"I'm sorry."

"She's pretty old. She sleeps by my bed."

"She must love you a lot."

He bites his lip and nods. Then he hugs me. "Thanks, cranberry."

He runs off.

I pass out more coupons. People like them, but here's what I'd like to pass out instead.

What I Learned This Summer by Anna McConnell

Pay attention to what's going on around you.
Trust your instincts.
If you see something, say something.
Don't be afraid to do something BIG.
Listen to people, really listen, and figure out how
    you can help.

Lorenzo taps his button: I'M WITH THE CRANBERRY.

But if I was wearing a button, I'd want mine to read: TELL ME.

Tell me what's going on with you.

Tell me what's wrong; how I can help.

Fred Dimsdale is talking to Dad.

"You've got a great girl there."

"I know."

I waddle over. Mr. Dimsdale says, "You seem older than when you left. You've added a new depth. Look at this crowd."

"I learned a lot this summer, sir."

"Use it, kid."

I will.

I go up to a sad-looking old man and bow. *How can I make you smile?*

That old man takes my hand and he twirls me around like we're on a dance floor, and I am thankful that my mother forced me to go to ballroom dancing for those six agonizing weeks.

People clap, and then he bows to me and he goes into the store.

Then I go up to my dad and bow. I take his hand.

"I don't dance, Anna."

He said this at the father/daughter dance.

"Try, Dad."

"Uh . . ."

"You just do this . . . see? "

Dad doesn't right off.

"No, look, you go one, two, three, one, two, three . . ."

Our dance isn't smooth like when I danced with the old man who knew the moves, but that's okay.

"Let's give it up for the cranberry and her father," Lorenzo shouts.

I smile at Dad and he grins at me.

And we dance in front of the Wide World of Cranberries store as the people applaud.

Epilogue

The day after my birthday, I thought I saw her at the grocery store.

A thin girl with straight, dark hair in a ponytail with a yellow scrunchie.

I ran up to her, but it wasn't Kim Su.

All last summer I kept her in my heart, hoping.

It's hard to turn that off; it's not like switching off a light and leaving a room.

I used to think that being brave happened instantly.

You take a big leap and don't look back.

But being brave also happens when you take small steps.

Even unsure steps.

Sometimes it takes a lot of courage to be who you are.

—Anna M. McConnell, age 13, Philadelphia

WITH THANKS TO:

- Marie Holm, a coordinator for women and girls at risk in Orange County, California, whose work gave me the seeds of the idea for this novel.

- Kally Reynolds, a coach and mentor to women at risk in Phoenix, Arizona, for her insights and inspiration.

- U.S. Immigration and Customs Enforcement, Department of Homeland Security, for their assistance in helping me authenticate this story.

- John Hurley, Artistic Director of the Ready, Set, Go Theater Company, who shared his experience training and loving horses.

- Jean Bauer (also known as my daughter), who helped me understand the connection between a horse and its human.

- Chris Blair, my assistant, who keeps things humming.

- Rita, Laura, and JoAnn, dear pals who never waiver.

And special thanks to Regina Hayes, my editor and friend.

TURN THE PAGE TO READ A SAMPLE OF
JOAN BAUER'S NEXT BOOK,

Soar

I'M PROBABLY TWELVE years old, that's what the doctors think. I could have been born anywhere, but it was most likely in Indianapolis, Indiana, at least that's where I've decided I was born because that's where I was found. Specifically, I was found at Computer Partners Inc. in the snack room right by the coffee pot. I think it's one of the reasons that I like the taste of coffee—it reminds me of home. I was found by Walt Lopper, a computer geek who had never so much as diapered a baby, but there I was and I'm told it was clear that I did need a new diaper. I needed a lot of other things, too, but my bottle wasn't empty so the police felt that meant I hadn't been there long. Walt found me at 7 a.m. on October 3rd—it was his turn to make coffee and he always got to work early. I was in my baby chair with a note.

pleez tek car of him Bcaz he my best boy
I no yur good!

There weren't any other clues about who left me there, but I'm inclined to believe it was my mother who might have worked nights cleaning office buildings. I had a little stuffed eagle that I was gnawing on, but other than that it was your usual thing. Walt called the police and they came and took me to the station and then someone from child services came and took me to a safe place, although Computer Partners was a safe place, real safe, otherwise my mother wouldn't have left me there. I'm told I didn't cry, I just watched people and took things in, but if you wanted to see what I was made of, try taking the stuffed eagle from my little hands. I'd yank it back and screech, "No!"

They think I was nine months old when I was found, so saying "no" is a pretty big deal. Walt said it indicated I had a big brain, possibly like Einstein. Walt has a big brain. He's officially a computer genius, but even bigger than his brain is his heart, which he said he hadn't paid that much attention to until I came along.

The police tried to find the person who left me. I

refuse to use the word abandoned because I'm fairly certain that my mother loved me and didn't have much choice but to leave me. I'm also fairly certain that she knew it was Walt's day to make the coffee. I think she probably checked out who was in that company and would never have left me there on a Monday, which was Dirk Dagwood's day to make coffee. From what I've heard, he might not even have noticed a baby sitting there chewing on a stuffed eagle. He was that kind of clueless.

It took awhile for Walt to adopt me, being a single man and all. He had to get trained and certified as a foster parent. It took another year of me living with him to convince the judge he should be my official dad. Walt spent a lot of time trying to figure me out, and I'm told he talked to me like I was a baby genius. He read me articles from computer magazines, he took computers apart and told me what he was doing and why. During baseball season we watched the games together and he told me how the pitcher was trying to psych out the batter and what some of the signals meant. My favorite signal involved tapping your nose, which Walt said could mean anything, depending on the day. I tapped my nose a lot and Walt carried me around explaining what everything was and how the world was a pretty complicated place, which I already knew.

When the adoption went through, Walt said, "It's official now. Okay?"

"Okay," I said. After that I started talking to Walt and to my stuffed eagle that I named Baby. I didn't talk to anyone else until later.

The problem with having a story like this is people don't know what to do with it. Their faces get super sad and their shoulders slump as they pat me on the head, which I find irritating, and say, "My, you are a little survivor, aren't you?"

Well, I suppose I am. But since I don't remember the first few years of my life, I don't feel like I can take any credit for it. And then there's the issue of my birthday, which is a theory, but schools seem to need an actual date, so I count three months ahead from October 3rd when I was found to early January. I give the doctor a fudge factor in his estimate of one week, which puts my birthday on January 10th. Getting close is important to me.

I've lived in four different places because Walt is a consultant and has to move around a lot. At my last two schools my class was learning the recorder. I'm so done with this instrument. I can play "Go Tell Aunt Rhody" in my sleep. I told Eddie Bartok, who was failing recorder, to pretend he was a snake charmer— they play instruments like this and get the snakes to dance up to the music. This caused Eddie to practice like crazy, but his mother wouldn't get him a snake. He tried charming worms in the garden, but worms today, they could care less. He played "Go Tell Aunt Rhody" to his dog who yelped and ran away. Once Eddie was at my house with his recorder and he tried to charm Baby.

"Inanimate things don't respond!" I mentioned.

And anyway, nobody can charm an eagle.

You can't keep an eagle in a cage or have one for a pet.

The number one rule for eagles is they have to be free.

I'm sure this is why my mother gave me that stuffy. She knew I had an eagle inside of me. Not everybody does.

But when you do, you'd better pay attention and deal with it, because if you don't, you'll have one intensely frustrating life.

Chapter

2

"I HAVE A new consulting gig," Walt tells me. "They pay up front."

This is excellent news because lots of Walt's clients take forever to pay him. Walt has his own consulting company, the Magellan Group. It's not a group, exactly, and no one is named Magellan; it's named after Ferdinand Magellan, our favorite dead-for-centuries explorer, who, like Walt, worked 24/7.

"Where is it?" I ask.

"Ohio."

We're living in St. Louis and I really, really like it here.

"The contract is for sixty days, Jer. It's kind of an emergency."

Everything Walt does is somebody's emergency. No

one calls my father and says, "Hey, all systems are go here. Just wanted you to know."

"Where in Ohio?" I ask.

"Near Cincinnati, but I don't think—"

"The Cincinnati Reds are looking strong this year, Walt." They're my third favorite team.

"They are, but I don't think—"

"The name of the town, Walt . . ."

"A smaller place than Cincinnati. Hillcrest, Ohio."

"They have a hill with a crest, right?"

Walt laughs. "Maybe. They have a company there and . . ."

The "and" part is always . . . "and they need a little help." Believe me, when Walt Lopper gets called in, it's because people need a lot of help.

"They've got a little problem, Jer."

"What kind of problem?"

"Their robots keep falling down."

"Why?"

"It's unclear."

I look in the corner. "Jerwal, are you awake?"

Jerwal, the robot Walt and I built together, glows and beeps.

Walt hasn't thought about taking any out of town business for a long time because of my heart. Four years ago, I had a perfectly healthy heart. Then something called cardiomyopathy happened and everything changed.

I look at Walt who sat with me every day I was in the hospital, who never once made me feel like I wasn't his kid, or any kind of disappointment, or a drain on his life.

"When do you have to be there?"

"Yesterday, Jer."

Today is March 27th and lots is about to happen here.

The Cardinals Opening Day is April 12th and we have tickets.

The science fair at my school is on April 27th and I'm working on a project that shows the trajectory of a well-hit baseball in 3D. I was thinking about contacting the manager of the St. Louis Cardinals to come see it—my findings could be big.

I take a deep breath and pull out my phone. Research is critical to decision making.

"Hillcrest, Ohio," I read to him. "Population 21,882, located in Ohio's rich farmland, in the western part of the state. A small midwestern town known for the excellence of its high school baseball program." This is getting interesting. "The Hillcrest High School Hornets have won six state championships and twice clinched the nationals." I look up. "We can gorge ourselves on baseball, Walt!"

Walt's face has that half-sunk look it gets when he hasn't told me everything.

"I think, Jer . . . well . . . I called your aunt Charity—"

"No."

"Let me finish. I called her and she said she would stay here with you so you could finish school—"

"No!"

"I want you to stay near Dr. Feinberg."

"There are doctors in Cincinnati."

"Wonderful doctors, no doubt."

"Do you care about my heart, Walt?"

"What kind of a question is that?"

An unfair question.

"She treats me like I'm a little kid!"

"I think if we talk to her—"

"We've done that. Aunt Charity smothers me." I feel my face get hot. "She makes me wash my hands hundreds of times."

"You are supposed to avoid infection, my man."

"Walt, please. I don't need to be a fanatic about

it." I squirt antiseptic goo on my hands and rub it in, counting to ten. "She asks me every morning"—I can hardly say it—"if I've had a bowel movement!"

"That's a tough one, Jer, but we do need to make sure all systems are go." He laughs at his joke.

"And do I have to even mention that she forced me against my will to make angel ornaments with little puffy skirts?"

Walt shakes his head, "I know. But she's been here for us. She's really helped out."

Aunt Charity stayed with us for six months when I was in and out of the hospital. I'm totally grateful she did this.

"She's my only sister. What can I tell you?"

"You can tell me she's not coming and I can go with you. I love her, okay? I just can't live with her right now." Possibly ever.

Walt stands up. "It's only for sixty days. What could happen?"

Phone again. I look up Shortest Wars in History. There's lots of material here. "Whole wars have been fought in less that thirty days, Walt. Can you really take the chance?"

Walt sips his coffee and looks at the map of the

ancient world that I gave him for his birthday. It shows how wrong they were back in the 1500s. This was what Magellan had to deal with. Despite all that, he circumnavigated the globe before people knew it was a globe.

Is that vision, or what?

"You're telling me, Jer, you want to leave sixth grade at the end of March and come with me to Hillcrest, Ohio, where I will be working day and night?"

I nod.

"What would you be doing there?" Walt persists.

"Gaining brilliance?"

"You're already too smart."

"I'd go to school and I'd help you. I could make dinner and—"

Walt shakes his head. His beard is getting some gray in it. People say it makes him look distinguished. He's wearing the T-shirt I got him for Father's Day—it has a mug of coffee and underneath that, the words: GAME CHANGER.

It's kind of our story.

"Jerwal," I say, "come forward." Jerwal moves slowly toward us. "Would you like to help the robots who are falling down?"

Jerwal has no idea, but he likes hearing his name. It took us months to get the voice-activated part working. We had to shorten his name because he couldn't understand "Jerwalthian," as in The Jerwalthian has entered the atmosphere.

Walt sips more coffee. "I'm sorry about how I live. I want you to have a stable environment."

"I don't feel unstable, Walt."

"You know what I mean. Not so much change."

"You don't change."

He laughs. "You're referring to my wardrobe?"

Walt wears blue shirts with jeans or khakis most days.

I stretch out my arms like I'm flying. "So we just swoop into Hillcrest and make it happen."

Walt sips coffee, thinking.

I sip decaf. "Jerwal, do you want to go play with the robots in Ohio?" Jerwal beeps and moves his head and arms from side to side. Walt points a finger of ultimate authority at me.

"To even consider it, Jer, and I'm not saying I am, Dr. Feinberg needs to sign off on this one hundred percent. You understand that might not happen."

I clear my throat. "I understand that in any contest,

I will be tested, maybe to the boundaries of my ability. And when this happens, I will remember that I have overcome great things already, and all that strength is in me."

Walt sniffs. "Which coach said that?"

"I just created it."

"Not bad."

When I'm a coach I'm going to tell my players to say that. I write it down.

Walt studies my face.

"I'm fine, Walt."

I say that a lot because it's true.

It's got to be true.

Foster McFee dreams of one day having her own cooking show. Her friend Macon wants to be a documentary filmmaker. And neighbor Miss Charleena plans a triumphant return to Hollywood. In fact, everyone in the tiny town of Culpepper seems to have a dream. But when some unexpected events shake up the town, the residents realize that sometimes the most important thing is having a big heart.

"A guaranteed feel-good story." —*Booklist*

"Tastier than a batch of Foster's triple chocolate cupcakes."
—*School Library Journal*